Historical Fiction:
A Rancher's Request -
A Victorian
American Western
by E. Ayers

Historical Fiction:
A Rancher's Request -
A Victorian American Western
by E. Ayers
Published by Indie Artist Press
Brackettville, Texas
www.indieartistpress.com
First Print Edition
copyright © 2017
All rights reserved.
ISBN-13: 978-1-62522-109-4
September 2017

This is a work of fiction. Creed's Crossing is fictional. Names, places, businesses, characters, and incidents are either the product of the author's imagination or are used in a fictitious manner. Any resemblance to actual persons living or dead, actual events or locales is purely coincidental. Franklin, Virginia is an actual town, and quite lovely, however the author has taken license with some geographical and other information surrounding the history and other facts relating to it.

Praise for A Rancher's Woman
Creed's Crossing Historical
Book 1

"These are men and women who jump off the page... This the BEST historical novel I have read in a long time... A total joy to read!"
Deb Morgan, Amazon Review, 5 STARS

"My husband was an American Indian. So, I was in awe of this story... Ms. Ayers, thank you for sharing this story. I will always remember this book and look forward to rereading it again."
Tarri, Amazon Review, 5 STARS

"...this story was beautifully written and the characters are unforgettable in this historical piece! Well done!"
rhollandl, Amazon Review, 5 STARS

"This was one of the more exciting historical stories due to the fact that Ms Ayers did so much research...it is definitely a 5 star book."
Kywoman, Amazon Review,

To George, who believed in me.

Part One

Zadie walked up the steep hill from the Blackwater River. In one hand, she carried her canvas satchel that contained her paints and several sketches, and her other hand curled around the frame of her oil painting. The sky was taking on shades of gold, peach, and pink. That meant she'd be late for, or had already missed, her dinner. Abilene would fuss, setting off a chain reaction. Zadie's mom would chime in and complain bitterly, and if her dad were home, he'd be furious with her, too. For some reason, he was protective of Abilene. The older woman had light-brown skin and soft dark waves that framed her face before being pulled into a tight bun at the nape of her neck. She did all of the cooking and housekeeping, and according to Zadie's mom, Abilene had been with Zadie's father's family since the beginning of time. And if anyone upset Abilene, they were in serious trouble with Zadie's father. But part of Zadie didn't care that she was late, that Abilene would complain, or that her father would be livid. She was too excited to eat.

Two egrets had posed in their mating plumage on the far side of the Blackwater River against the grassy bank. Seeing them was spectacular, and having them prance around long enough to sketch them dressed in their finest had been a rare opportunity. Satisfaction welled and made the uphill walk

A Rancher's Request

to her parents' house worth the effort, even if she was walking into yet another admonishment for being tardy to supper. This would make the third time this week she was late.

She walked up Second Avenue, turning once to look over the city below her, and then to her house at the top of the rise. Five chimneys flanked her house, as though anchoring it on top of the hill. As she went up the stone path to the door, white lace billowed from her bedroom windows on the second floor. All she wanted was to quietly slip into the house and up the front stairs to her room where she could unpack her paints and organize her sketches. Gathering all of her art supplies into one hand, she gently pressed down the latch on the front door of the white and gray Greek revival she called home. The door's hinges made a tiny squeak as she entered and another squeak as she closed the door behind her. Picking up her skirt, she flew to the staircase and had managed to ascend several steps before knocking the edge of her painting against a stair.

"Zadie, is that you I hear?"

She grimaced at the sound of her father's deep voice. "No, Poppa, it is a great black bear that has come to visit."

"Do you think you are too old to have your father wash your mouth with soap?"

She let out a sigh. "Poppa, I was only jesting. You knew it was me, making your question as ridiculous as my answer."

"I have no desire to holler across the house. Come into my office at once."

"Please, Poppa, allow me to put my things away and wash my hands and face so that I am presentable." Failing to wait for his answer, she scurried to her room.

A few minutes later, feeling refreshed yet

A Rancher's Request

hesitant to listen to his tirade, she wandered into her father's office. "Hello, Poppa."

"You missed your dinner."

Her stomach tightened as she took a seat and waited for his reprimand.

He picked up a piece of paper and waved it in the air. "I have a letter from Reginald Lorde. His son has gone to Wyoming to start his own ranch." Her father shook his head. "Why that blasted young man would go and do a darn thing like that is beyond me, but he has. Now he's written home requesting a bride."

Zadie's chest tightened and the nape of her neck prickled. "Poppa, you wouldn't."

"You've had things around here your way for the last five years. I sent you to that fancy ladies' college. And what have you done since you've returned home?" He lifted his eyebrows. "Nothing other than paint a few pictures and tutor a handful of children in the fine art of drawing."

"But--"

"No. "He raised his hand so that his palm faced her. "There will be no discussion. Your mother and I have talked about it. You will marry this man."

Anger flowed through every limb, heating her body as tears formed. "You're going to send me off to some god-forsaken territory in the west as though I were a piece of chattel to be sold?"

"No. I have arranged a good marriage for you. Duncan Lorde is a fine man from a wealthy family. So far, you've ignored every suitor, and I can't say I blame you. You deserve someone worth marrying. This way is best."

Tears threatened to spill as she rose from the chair by her father's desk. She ran out of his office, up the staircase, and to her bedroom where she threw herself across her bed and sobbed.

"Zadie, wake up. When did you last eat?"

Zadie forced her eyes open at the sound of her mother's voice. The memory of her father's proposal hit her about the same time as her head began to pound with each pulse of her blood. "Oh, Momma. Do you know what Poppa intends to do?"

"Yes, my darling. It is a good match." She patted Zadie's arm. "My parents arranged my marriage to your father, and I couldn't have asked for a better man."

Zadie knitted her brow. "You and Poppa?"

"Oh, yes. He was graduating from medical school and planning on settling here. My father was nothing more than an oysterman with a few boats. I couldn't believe my good fortune."

"But you and Poppa are so much in love."

Zadie's mother laughed. "I was excited and scared at the same time. Then I met him.

How could I not fall in love with a man who has eyes that are so dark they remind me of the darkest summer night?"

Zadie looked at her mother. "Momma, I can't marry some man I don't know."

"Duncan's father has been a good friend for many years."

"Then why have I not heard of this family?"

"Because they live in North Carolina. Your grandfather knew them and that is how your father knows them."

Zadie shook her head.

"Now, drink some tea and eat a biscuit with the wonderful mulberry jam Abilene made this morning."

"Momma, I refuse to have my father ship me off to some horrible place to marry a man that I do not know."

"You will obey your father. You have no say in the matter. He loves you dearly and

A Rancher's Request

only wants what is best for you. Trust him."

***

Duncan rode his horse, Rocky, along the barbed wire fence line of his property. His land purchase had given him a fair chunk of good prairie, and the south end of his property touched the road leading to the town of Creed's Crossing. Last year, he'd spent his summer planting an orchard not far from his house and creating farmland out of grassland. This year he could see the fruits of his labor.

His original herd of fifty red Angus cows was about to almost double in size from the looks of the fat bellies of those females. And once those young calves dropped, he'd be busy. Unfortunately, he had no help. He was barely making it financially, and the thought of hiring someone gave him a chill. He patted the neck of his stallion and the large horse responded by twitching his ears.

Duncan rode along for another few hundred yards, and when he reached a crest, he spotted an encampment of Indians who had cut a section of his fence. Why?

He knew enough to know that his anger wouldn't serve him well. Why must you take my fence down? He nudged his heels into Rocky and the stallion responded with a hasty gallop. Duncan reined the horse in as he entered the encampment. The scent of meat cooking made him wonder if he'd lost one of his cattle to the Indians, too.

It didn't take Duncan more than a minute to ascertain that the tribe was Lakota. Duncan blew out a breath and looked for what he thought might be the chief's tent.

A young man stepped in front of Rocky. "Why you here?"

A Rancher's Request

"You are on my land."

"This our land." The Indian frowned.

"My land is fenced."

"No. You put fence on our land."

Duncan wanted to choke the Lakota. Instead Duncan swallowed his anger. "Where is your chief?"

The young man pointed to a tent.

Duncan rode his horse to the tipi and dismounted. He'd heard plenty of stories about what the Indians did to white people, but he refused to show his fear. Yet that little doubt crept up his spine as he entered a large tent.

He blinked several times, trying to adjust his eyesight to the darkness inside the massive building made from hides and poles. Several older men sat together on the far side of the tipi, while three women appeared to be cooking over an open fire in the center. A young woman tended two small children and another woman held an infant.

Duncan nodded at the women as he approached the older men. "Excuse me. Who do I need to speak to about the fact that your people cut my fence and are now camping on my land?"

A wrinkled old man cleared his throat before speaking. "Are you the person who put fences on our hunting grounds? Land that was given to us by your government."

"What do you mean by your land? I paid for this land."

"Then it is best you sit and learn, for you have fenced our land. Land that was given to us in a treaty."

Several hours later, Duncan walked out of the tent. They had been kind and even fed him a meal of elk. He'd only asked that in the future they not destroy his fence, crops, or take his cattle. They'd agreed, and Duncan

A Rancher's Request

was certain they would uphold their promise.

Duncan patted his mount. "Okay, Rocky, let's go home. I've had enough for one day."

Life was lonely. Conversing with Rocky wasn't the same as talking to a person. He wanted a bride. "A sweet temperament." He looked up at the blue sky and then off to the west where the mountains reached for the sky. There was plenty left to do before the sun began to vanish behind those mountains. "Surely would be nice if she can cook and be easy on the eyes."

He'd been told about the mail order brides, and a few men got lucky, but he had decided he was better off trusting his father to find him a suitable woman. He plodded his way home, as thoughts of canned beans, the Indian encampment, acreage that needed to be plowed, and beautiful women played in his mind. Find me a good woman, Dad.

E. Ayers

Three days later, Duncan rode into Creed's Crossing and found a letter from his father awaiting him. As soon as he returned home, he opened the letter and read it.

Dearest son,

I contacted an old friend of mine, Gregory Larkford. Our fathers were long-standing friends, and I've known Gregory as far back as I can remember. Gregory became a doctor about the same time as I opened the herring packing plant. I'll be honest and say I've not seen his daughter in quite a few years, but she was a cute little girl with dark brown hair and dark eyes like her father. I know she's an intelligent thing and went to a college for women. Gregory has agreed to the marriage of his daughter.

A smart woman can be good, but she can also create problems. I have no

A Rancher's Request

idea if she's been fed a bunch of nonsense about women's rights. Our newspapers are filled with stories of women demanding equal rights. Women need to stop the twaddle and stay home with their babies.

I believe Gregory will send a letter to you shortly. I know he has some questions for you. It is best that you answer truthfully and do not embellish.

Is your house ready for a woman?

With love,

Father

Duncan looked around his place. It was nice and tight with well-chinked walls. It had only three rooms, but that was enough. The whole place was smaller than the parlor in the house where he'd grown up. This cabin is enough. This isn't the big city, so why would a woman need more?

E. Ayers

***

Zadie wanted to return to the spot where the river made a deep curve with the hopes of seeing the egrets again. But her mother had other plans for her. Since Abilene did all the cooking, Zadie had never been taught. Now she was being forced to stand beside Abilene to learn everything about cooking and running a household. At college, she acquired a few basics out of dire necessity, but what she was being taught by Abilene went beyond washing out her undergarments. After only two days of this nonsense, her hands were red and raw, and her nails were chipped. This whole situation is only going to get worse. How will I survive this?

Ironing was the worst. The heavy iron made her arm ache, and if she wasn't careful, she'd scorch something else. She'd already

A Rancher's Request

ruined her father's favorite white shirt. It now carried an ugly burn near the cuff. And another distasteful chore was filleting fish. She hated the texture of the skin and all the scales that clung to her fingers and splattered on her apron. Abilene saved all the heads to make a fish broth. Why must I think about my food having eyes?

She had notes on planting vegetables and herbs and a ton of recipes. Learning to make vermicelli, croquets, and polenta was almost fun, and roasting turkey, chicken and other fowl was easy, until she'd discovered she'd have to remove the feathers herself. Boiling ham wasn't too bad, nor was making stews. Baking took practice, but she enjoyed it in spite of the fact that a few of her attempts were not edible and could have been used as cannon ammunition. And as the days grew warmer, she hated being in the kitchen with its hot stove. Even though the kitchen had been moved to a small open building in the backyard, it was still hot as Hades. Perspiration often ran into her eyes and her clothes clung to her body like wet sheets, making her feel twice as warm.

Zadie's mom let her take the day off after she had attended church on Sunday. Zadie gathered her sketchpad and flew down the hill to the river, searching its banks for the egrets.

She looked in each direction and finally gave up. After placing her satchel on the ground, she spread a blanket, and carefully sat. She scanned the water and hoped to find some sort of wildlife to sketch. A robin tweeted and a Carolina wren flicked its upturned tail as it skittered into a nearby bush. That's not what she wanted. She wanted those egrets to reappear. With a deep sigh, she leaned back on the blanket, blocked the sun from her eyes

A Rancher's Request

with her hand, and looked up. Thin white clouds covered most of the pale blue sky. The sun beat down on her, and moisture beaded on her forehead and most of her body.

Catherine Duke's twins ran past, giggling with their carefree childhood abandon. And Catherine called to them with the desperate plea of a mother who was tired of chasing them. Some part of Zadie smiled, happy not to be a mother on such a hot day. Movement in the trees across the water caught her attention. She sat up and peered into the copse. Then she saw what she wanted. The egrets had made a nest high up in a Cyprus tree. Yes! She took out her sketchpad and began to draw.

The twins ran past again, squealing and alerting every creature in the area. Several birds took flight. Zadie wanted to laugh at the noisy twins who seemed to be enjoying their outing, but she was afraid they might scare away the egrets before she could finish her sketch.

"Hello," Catherine said as she approached. "Mind if I join you? I love watching you draw. "

Zadie forced a smile. "Not at all."

Catherine sat on the corner of the blanket. "I hope the children aren't disturbing you. Living with John's family isn't easy. I'm constantly trying to keep the children quiet. They need a chance to run and play."

"I thought you were getting your own place?" Zadie asked her longtime friend and former childhood playmate.

"We are hoping John becomes a supervisor this month at the sawmill. Then we'll have enough money. There's a house on Clay Street that we've looked at and drooled over."

"Mrs. Baxley's?"

"Yes. Since Mrs. Baxley died, the family is looking to sell it. The nearest son lives in

A Rancher's Request

Windsor and doesn't want it."

"That's what I heard." Zadie continued to sketch as she chatted. "It's a lovely little house."

"It's enough for us. We've been saving for this. Wait until you marry. You'll discover how difficult it is to budget."

A shiver ran up her spine. "Marriage isn't that far off for me."

"*You* have a suitor?"

"Thank you very much. You make it sound as though I would never have one."

Catherine looked at her children who were now tossing seeds from a maple tree into the air and watching them spin to the ground. "I didn't mean it that way. But you never seem to have an interested male. You went off and were educated. This is Franklin. No one around here does that."

"Well, I did and I'm glad I did. And as for my suitor, he's the son of an old family friend."

She decided that wasn't lying. It also wasn't telling the whole truth.

"Oh, that's so exciting. Tell me more! Do I know him?"

She shook her head. "Not much to tell. He's from Edenton, he's moved to Wyoming, and we've been corresponding. So far everything is going well." All right, that's a lie. Maybe I should write to him. What if this doesn't work?

"Oh, I'm so happy for you."

"Well, don't get your hopes up or spread a bunch of gossip, because I still don't know what will happen. We'll leave it with so far everything is working well." Another lie. If you call getting chapped hands from all the laundry as working well, it's a fry-in-Hell sort of lie. I'd like to skewer my father and roast him for dinner.

"Wyoming? Isn't that a territory?"

A Rancher's Request

Zadie shook her head. "It recently gained statehood."

"Aren't there Indians out there?"

Again, Zadie nodded. "I've heard it is very wild in the west."

"Aren't you scared?"

Zadie smiled. I'm scared out of my skin and not so much about the Indians. I'm more worried about my own survival skills without a maid to help me. "I'm certain Duncan will protect me."

"Promise you won't leave here without telling me, as you did that year when you spent almost the whole summer with your aunt."

"I promise." Zadie frowned at her friend. "I was eight at the time. I have grown up. Besides I think my mother wants to have a big party for me."

"Oh, a party. I love parties. Except this party will mean you are going away. What will

I do without my dear friend?"

"You will be forced to write letters. And I'll expect one weekly."

"Weekly? When will I find the time?"

Zadie couldn't stop the giggle that rose in her throat like a hundred bubbles. "It will give you an excuse to have a few minutes to yourself." She pressed her lips together. "I wish I could cross the river and climb that tree. I want to see the eggs that the egret has laid."

"Are you daft? It's swampy on the other side."

Zadie shrugged. Catherine will never understand. I wonder if Duncan Lorde will? Or does he expect me to be the good wife by producing a baby for him every two years, fixing all of his meals, cleaning his house, and slopping the pigs, while he plays poker with the men every Friday night in some saloon? Warnings of such things were often found in the religious tracts left around the college campus.

A Rancher's Request

After spending most of the afternoon by the water visiting with Catherine, Zadie came home and went to her room. I've put it off long enough. I need to write to him.

She pulled a sheet of paper from her stationery box and sat at her desk. Uncapping her ink, she began to think about what she might write. No point in making it flowery. Then she had to decide if she was going to call him by his formal name or his familiar one. Formal.

Dear Mr. Lorde,

I decided it was best if I write directly to you and tell you a few things about myself. There is no point in my coming out there if you don't like me. So I will be blunt.

I have been told that I'm pretty, but I believe that I am average. I've seen plenty of women who are by far prettier and plenty who are quite plain. I'm someplace in the middle. My hair is dark brown, almost black, and my eyes are also very dark, but my skin is fair. I'm also somewhat thin, and unfortunately, I lack the generous curves of most women.

I have been educated in the arts at State Female Normal School, in Farmville, Virginia, and I am qualified to teach. I would prefer to teach art rather than mathematics.

I have no interest in marrying a man who cannot accept me as an intellectual equal. The thought of running a household, fixing meals, et cetera, has little appeal, but I am willing to do it. But please don't ask me to slop pigs. Certainly, we can divide responsibilities into comfortable and appropriate allotments without assigning chores by what is often delegated by gender.

A Rancher's Request

She wrote a few more sentences, and then reviewed what she'd written. Satisfied, she folded the letter, placed it in an envelope, and glued it closed. *That should scare him.*

***

With calves dropping daily, Duncan didn't dare take off for town. Calves in the morning, plowing and seeding in the afternoon, I have no time for anything else. Having worked fishing boats and their nets, he had plenty of upper body strength. But nothing had prepared him for the strength he needed on his own ranch, holding a plow behind his mule, Nellie, or the hours spent in a saddle. By the time night came, he barely had strength to fix a can of beans before tumbling into bed. His thoughts of a pretty woman with a nice meal awaiting him and sleeping at his side were the only things on his mind, as he'd close his eyes each night. Then dawn would break much too soon, and he'd drag himself from bed and start over. Knowing his only real meal would be breakfast, he fixed eggs and bacon, or he'd slice a bit of ham depending on which meats he'd bought.

His hectic pace meant he'd missed going to town on Friday. Now he was out of meat with only one egg left. He was forced to go to town because he was also out of beans. Sighing, he fried the last egg.

In the early morning light, as the stars began to fade, it didn't take him long to saddle Rocky for the short ride, which barely took an hour. When he pulled in front of the farm supply, they had not yet opened. The entire town was quiet. He blew an impatient breath from between pursed lips. There was nothing he could do but wait.

A Rancher's Request

He looked up at the sky and realized he could no longer see stars, but he also didn't see a blue sky. Instead the sky was taking on shades of red and pink. Oh no, I don't need rain this morning.

The mercantile door opened and the owner's wife stepped outside. He watched as she began to sweep the wooden porch, and then rode his horse there. "Good morning, are you open?"

Mrs. Barrett smiled. "We certainly are. What would you like today?"

"I'd really like some breakfast. Eggs, ham, and something to eat other than beans. I'm sick of beans."

Mrs. Barrett laughed. "Duncan, either you need to learn to cook, or you need to find a wife. Can you boil potatoes?"

He shrugged. "Just potatoes? I assume so."

She rolled her eyes at him. "I'm going to

give you some cabbage, green beans, and then you need to go to the butcher for a nice piece of corned beef to go with the potatoes. Listen carefully."

He followed her inside.

Her directions seemed simple, and she wrote each step down as she told him. At least he could eat for several days from one pot. She told him how to cut the potatoes for frying in the morning. It seemed easy enough, but he wasn't certain how he'd find the time. I need a wife.

2

Duncan paid for the food items from the mercantile, purchased corned beef from the butcher, and then went to the farm supply where he picked up the piece he needed for his plow. By then, the bakery was open and he bought a loaf of bread, a half-dozen biscuits, and treated himself to a dozen sticky cinnamon and raisin rolls, along with a few cookies.

His last stop was the tiny post office. He had several letters from home, but one letter with a flourished script came from Franklin,

Virginia. He pocketed all the letters and decided he'd wait until he was home to read them. He needed to outrun the storm.

Not far from his cabin, the first drop of rain pelleted him, then another and another. He gave Rocky a nudge and Rocky went into a full gallop. They were drenched by the time they reached the barn.

Duncan settled his horse before making his way to his cabin. Opening the door, he encountered the water on the floor where it had come through the open window. One more thing in my day that is not going well. First I get soaked and now this? He left his packages on the table and grabbed his dirty clothes to mop up the water. If I'm stuck inside, I might as well do my laundry. With the worst of the water soaked into his clothes, he pulled off his wet shirt and tossed it with the others. From the shelf near his bed, he lifted the last pair of clean pants he owned and left the last clean shirt where it was. He certainly didn't need to be dressed to do his laundry. Then he tossed a few pieces of wood into his stove and began to heat some water. While he waited on the water, he unwrapped his food items. The way they'd been bundled, the only things that had become wet were his sweet sticky buns and the paper that held the corned beef.

If he cooked the beef right away, the water wouldn't matter, and certainly he could eat a dozen slightly waterlogged buns before the day was finished. One cookie was also a little damp. He shoved that cookie into his mouth as he poured the hot water into the washtub.

By the time he'd finished doing his laundry, his stomach was loudly protesting. He sat at his table and ate three of the cinnamon raisin buns and washed them down with leftover coffee that had been there since morning. He loved those sweet treats more than anything he could remember eating at home. Sorry, Mom. Even soggy, these are the best.

It was then it dawned on him that he had letters from home. He had tossed them on his bed as he had gathered his laundry. Collecting them, he chose to first read the flourished handwriting from Franklin, Virginia. From my future bride?

He opened each piece of mail and spread out the damp pages on his table, and then poured the last bit of coffee into his cup. The cabin was hot from the stove, so he opened the front door, hoping that the roof over the porch was enough to keep the deluge of water from entering.

Raindrops hitting his metal roof told him when the rain had eased up and when it returned to a full downpour. His parents had a standing seam roof, and he remembered hearing the dissonance of rain on the roof. But his childhood home had an attic to deaden the sound, and this cabin had nothing to suppress the cacophony. He covered his ears and realized it did nothing for the situation.

Perspiration ran down his chest and soaked the waistband of his pants. He downed that last bit of coffee and made another pot. Pumping another pan full of water, he added the corned beef. He figured he might as well fix the meat. It certainly wasn't going to get any cooler anytime soon.

Satisfied, he picked up the one letter written in an elegant script and sat on the bench on the front porch. Rain sheeted off the roof and onto the ground. He lifted the scalloped page to his nose and sniffed. "Humph." Not even the slightest scent of perfume. "I thought women were supposed to scent their letters."

The rain had caused the ink to bleed on the page, but it was still very legible. He read the note, and when he reached the part about her refusal to slop the pigs, he couldn't stop his laughter. As his composure returned, he read the rest of his letters. As usual, his mother missed him. And his father's note was brief, but mostly about herring and the number of pounds per day that had been caught. The only other letter that captured his interest was from Dr. Gregory Larkford, promising his daughter's hand in marriage.

Zadie was apparently spoiled, but from the father's letter, she was learning how to manage a household and do the associated chores. The father also spoke about his daughter's talent. Apparently she was quite gifted.

Duncan went inside and checked on the stove. He fixed another cup of coffee and then found his box that contained pen and paper. So many times while plowing he'd given thought to how he might woo his bride. But after reading the letter from her father and Zadie's own letter, all thoughts of pressing and sending her the pretty orange and yellow flowers that grew in the fields left his mind. She wasn't going to be impressed with a few dead flowers.

He stifled his laughter and figured he could give what he'd received from her. He opened his box of stationery, withdrew a sheet of paper, opened his inkbottle, and dipped the nib of his pen into the liquid.

Dear Miss Zadie Larkford,
I don't own any pigs.
Sincerely,
Mr. Duncan Lorde

***

E. Ayers

Zadie found herself looking forward to Sunday afternoons, as that was the only time she had to herself these days. So when she unexpectedly had a moment on Wednesday afternoon, she slipped away from the house and went to find Ole Bill. He was an older Negro who often frequented the docks, hoping to pick up a job for a few pennies. At other times, he could be found in town, doing some job for a merchant. He did the jobs that no one else would do.

She found him fishing. His gray hair and beard were distinctive.

"Ole Bill," she called.

"Yessum, Miz Larkford. What canna do for yous?"

"I don't need you today, but Sunday afternoon, I have a request. Will you take me across the water and bring your ladder?" She smiled sweetly. "I'd like to climb to that branch, right there." She pointed to the Cyprus tree.

"Why yous wanna do a fool ding like dat?"

"I want to see into the nest up there."

"Daz gonna peck yous brains outta yous head."

"I hope not." She gave him her best smile and dropped a few coins into his hand. "I'll see you Sunday afternoon." She started to walk away, and then turned back to him. "Don't say a word to my father."

Ole Bill was one of the trustworthiest men in town. His kinky hair told her he was a Negro, and his skin had become tanned like an old piece of leather left on the side of a barn for too long. The man chuckled. "I ain't gonna says a word."

She had probably spent too much time looking for Ole Bill, so she hurried to the post office where she found not one letter but two

E. Ayers

from Duncan Lorde, except one was addressed to her father. Where will I find it later? His desk drawer. I'll be certain to clean his office tomorrow once he's left the house.

A dress in the window of Ethel's shop caused her to stop. The bodice and skirt were made from pure white cotton, and the sleeves were made of gauze. Trimmed in eyelet lace, it was lovely. She pushed open the door and entered the dark interior. Blinking several times, her eyes still had not adjusted when Ethel called to her.

"Miss Larkford, what brings you in here today?"

Zadie turned in the direction of the voice. "That beautiful white dress, but... I'm thinking... I'm going to need several new outfits."

"You? You must have a wardrobe filled with lovely dresses."

"Oh, I do, but I'm going to need things

that will be more practical for everyday wear. I'm... Ah, I'm not exactly certain when, but I believe before the end of summer, I'll be moving."

"Have you taken a job at a grand school?"

Zadie's eyes had adjusted, and she could now see Ethel Kern and all the fabrics inside the narrow store on Main Street. Zadie forced a slight smile. "I might be getting... We're working on the details." She hated her fair skin and knew she was blushing. "Married."

"Well, that is exciting news. Who is the lucky man?"

"The son of a family friend. I've never met him, but we've been corresponding. He's living in Wyoming."

"Oh, my! Aren't you afraid? There are Indians there."

"I try not to think about them. Most of them live on reservations now, and the ones that aren't, the Army is supposed to hunt them down and then place them back on the reservations." Zadie realized her words made those people sound like tigers in a zoo that had broken free. She returned to the subject of dresses. "I came because I love that dress in your window and would love to have one like it."

"I made it as a sample, but you are welcome to try it on." Ethel walked to the dress form. "It just might fit you."

Zadie tried not to show her enthusiasm, but she had fallen madly in love with the simple white dress. She took the dress Ethel handed her, stood behind the screen at the back of the store, and slipped into the summery frock. It barely needed anything more than a few buttons moved.

Ethel smiled broadly. "I think I must have made it just for you." She made a few chalk marks. "Just lovely."

"I was thinking about some other dresses. Nothing fancy, just day dresses. I was really thinking ahead to some things for this fall and winter. And maybe some pretty aprons."

"Well, it's never too soon to start."

Zadie picked out several fabrics. "I believe I will need warm clothes in the winter, and I will need sturdy ones." She lifted a bolt of light brown twill. "Can you make a skirt from this? Something generous so that I can ride a horse?"

"Ride? There's... Let me find the pattern." Ethel dug through a pile of papers near her desk. "This is the rage in Europe."

"Pants?"

"Yes, but it looks like a skirt. It's split."

"Hmm." Zadie pondered and remembered her classmate from school who had family in Texas. She recalled what they wore there and how often they rode horses. "I can't imagine, but it seems as though it would make sense and certainly it would be practical for daily wear. And maybe slightly shorter...I don't want to be dragging the hem through snow or worse."

"My dear, Zadie. You sound as though you are taking a maid's job."

Zadie put her hand over her heart. "Oh, heavens, no! Don't say that. I've been told that people live very independently in these new frontier states." She looked around the shop. "I have no idea what to expect, but I want to be prepared." She squared her shoulders. "I am a strong, capable woman."

By the time she was finished, she'd chosen several items. Ethel wasn't going to bring in any new bolts of wool over the summer months, and what little she had left was only enough for a few vests. Zadie decided she could use the vests for extra warmth, and Ethel promised to send two wool skirts in the fall. She'd keep scraps from the vests so she could match the colors.

Satisfied, Zadie began walking home. Ethel wasn't the type of woman to wag her tongue, and Zadie knew whatever had been said would remain private. Judging from the sun, it probably wasn't much past two o'clock, yet perspiration beaded on her forehead. Summer is coming early.

With her house in sight, she trudged onward until she heard the sharp note of the mill's whistle. She turned and looked over the town below as the piercing sound faded. The whistle blew two more times in short blasts. That meant there had been an accident at the sawmill. Barely a week went by that someone wasn't hurt. Fortunately, it was rare that anyone was severely injured. Then she immediately thought about her friend Catherine and Catherine's husband John Duke. Oh, please, don't let anything happen to him. They are trying to buy that house and those twins need their father.

Zadie pulled Duncan Lorde's letter from her pocket as she walked up the hill to her home. Short and to the point, she laughed as she read it. Duncan, I already like you.

It was well past suppertime when her father returned home.

"Poppa, was John Duke hurt?"

"No. I doubt you know the man. It could have been worse. He'll be out of work for a while, but he'll heal just fine." He frowned. "Whatever made you think it was John who was hurt?"

"That name popped into my mind when I heard the whistle."

Her father shook his head as though she had lost hers. "Send Abilene to my office. I'm starved."

Relief flooded Zadie, and she wanted to know more, but her father said little about his patients. She leaned up and kissed his cheek before going in search of Abilene. Zadie helped prepare her father's tray. Then Abilene served him dinner in his office. Zadie retired to her room and decided to write to Duncan.

Dear Duncan,

It would help if you told me about your days. I only know a few things about life on the other side of the Mississippi. I'm being forced to make decisions without any basis. Will you please tell me how much snow to expect? And do you have a carriage for me or will I be riding astride a horse? (I do know how to ride.) Are there foxhunts and tea parties? Will I be expected to play golf or prepare dinner parties for your friends? Or is my life going to be filled with doing laundry, cooking, washing dishes, and scrubbing the floors like a maid, while simultaneously providing you a dozen babies?

Yours truly,

Zadie

***

Duncan surveyed his acreage. The Lakota Indians were still camped at the northern end of his property, but they seemed to be keeping their promises to him. He knew of several ranchers in the area who had no problem with these small bands of Indians that roamed freely, yet he'd also heard how destructive and dangerous they could be.

The prairie grass was thick after the wet spring, but it had been fairly dry since Duncan had planted his crops. He needed the rain or he'd lose them. The sun shone on the pale green sprouts, many of which already had yellowed edges.

Five Paws, a Lakota who had been camping on Duncan's property and had helped Duncan on several occasions, rode in his direction. He had a woman with him who Duncan assumed was Five Paws' wife. Duncan raised his hand in a wave and the couple joined him.

"Good morning."

Five Paws nodded. "We ride to creek and look for berries. You come?"

Duncan shook his head. "I need to go to town." The woman's eyes grew wide as he continued. "I need some supplies. I could go with you this afternoon. Berries would be a nice treat."

The woman said something to her husband and he shook his head. Her facial expression instantly turned sad, as though her husband had disapproved of her. Duncan had seen that look too many times on his mother's face when his father was unhappy. It weighed heavy on Duncan's heart. Maybe it was his mother's influence on him, but he had a soft spot when it came to women.

Duncan tore his gaze away from the couple for a moment, and then said, "Why don't you come back to the cabin with me, and then we can go into town together? I owe you much for helping me with my fields. Now would be a good time to repay you."

"Town with you?" Five Paws answered. "White man shoot us."

"You will be with me. There are other Indians who go into Creed's Crossing. The people there seem to accept Indians when they are accompanied."

The Indian cocked his head as though listening for something. "Accompanied?"

"It means you come with me." Duncan

nudged his horse. "But first, your wife must cover her…legs. White men are not supposed to see a woman's legs."

"What wrong with her legs?"

Duncan could feel the heat flowing to his cheeks. He would not have called the man's wife pretty, but there was nothing wrong with her limbs. He also wondered if she wore anything under her tunic.

When he arrived at his cabin, he had to search for the pair of pants he wanted. They would be huge on her, but they had quickly become too small for him. His leg muscles seemed to have doubled in size since he had started ranching. He found the pants and a length of rope. Then he was forced to try to explain pants to a woman who spoke virtually no English.

She put them on, and they fell to the floor. He then had her hold them up while he threaded the belt loops with rope, tightening between each loop. Several times his fingers accidentally touched her skin and he could feel the heat climbing to his cheeks. But as he tied the rope in front, he realized her stomach had a slight bulge. She was another man's wife and in a family way. Guilt grabbed his innards and twisted them. When he was done, he rolled the bottom of the pants so she could walk freely. She smiled at him as though he had dressed her like a queen. Another round of guilt swept through him, knotting his insides. He looked at Five Paws and nodded approval.

The men were ready to leave, but not the wife. She was busy touching everything in the kitchen. Duncan wanted to laugh, but he could see Five Paws becoming annoyed.

Finally Duncan turned and asked his friend what his wife's name was. The man knitted his brow and by the time he was done,

Duncan wasn't certain if it was Prairie Dog or Gopher. Neither name was suitable for a young woman.

They returned to their horses and left for town. With each passing moment, Duncan was feeling very protective of her, as though she were his younger sister. They had ridden along for several minutes when Duncan broke the silence. "When you say her name in your language, it sounds lovely, but not in ours. She needs a pretty name. I will call her Dora Grace."

Duncan decided she must have liked her new name because she smiled broadly when Five Paws spoke to her and she repeated her name.

In response to Rocky's gait, Duncan rocked in his saddle and eventually the town came into view. He looked over at Five Paws and knew the young man was tense from the way he pressed his lips together. But Dora Grace was as excited as a child on Christmas day. She was totally wide-eyed and smiling as she peered around her husband's back.

Slowly they walked their horses through the town to the farm supply store. Several people stopped and watched as they rode past. "Stay with me and don't make any quick movements. They've seen other Indians, but I believe they are leery."

"They no like us."

"They have reason to be concerned. But you are with me." They reached the front of the store and dismounted.

The three of them walked inside and Duncan knew Five Paws was admonishing his wife by the tone in his voice. Duncan felt sorry for her, yet understood her enthusiasm might be a problem.

Ted Barrett welcomed Duncan, and then looked at Five Paws. "You need something?"

Five Paws said nothing, as though he

didn't understand a word of English. Duncan motioned for the Indian to follow him. There were drawers filled with seeds for a vegetable garden, but Duncan really didn't know which seeds to purchase. "Do you have any suggestions for my kitchen garden?"

Five Paws said something to his wife and she stepped from behind him to the counter.

Duncan pointed to his chest. "For me."

He knew she did not read, so she must have known each seed by its size, shape, and color. She had him buying quite a few. Ted Barrett put each variety into a folded pouch of paper and marked the name on the paper. As they were finishing up, Ted's face drained of color when he seemed to look behind where Duncan was standing. Duncan turned and saw Five Paws playing with a hatchet. The Indian practically twirled it in his hand as though it were a baton.

A second later, a man walked through the door and yelled, "Drop it, Injun!"

Ted hollered, "No!"

A gun went off. Glass shattered. The man who had held the gun bellowed. The hatchet was buried in the frame of the front door. An old man who had been in the store, hurried to pick up the pistol that was still skittering across the floor. Taking Five Paws arm, Duncan yanked his friend out the back door.

Duncan took a few deep breaths and then relieved himself against a buttercup. "What just happened in there?"

Five Paws shrugged. "White men don't like us."

Duncan ran his fingertips over his forehead. "No wonder people are afraid of you. I've never seen anything to compare with what you just did. Never."

"Dora Grace?"

Blood was still pumping at high speed through Duncan's body as they stepped inside. Dora Grace was crouched near the seeds, and Ted Barrett was petting her head in some sort of attempt to calm her. Five Paws took his wife's hand and pulled her to her feet. Duncan walked to where the hatchet was in the doorframe and removed it.

"Ted, add this hatchet to my seeds." He pointed to the trapper who had entered the store. "That man can pay for the damage he caused."

Ted chuckled. "I hope your friend is always on the good side, because I'd hate to be up against him."

"His name is Five Paws, and if it wasn't for him, I wouldn't have managed to get everything done this spring. I can't do it all by myself. And Dora Grace is his wife. I think I'm going to have quite a vegetable garden this year."

"Are you going to keep them like the

Coleman's?"

Duncan turned to his friend. "We haven't discussed it, but I'd like to think they might stay."

Duncan walked out of the store and headed for the mercantile and its dry goods. He needed several things and knew Dora Grace would be in heaven in such a place. It didn't take but a few seconds for her eyes to widen, and then she was either looking at or touching something in the store. But when she saw the ladies' dresses, she raised her eyebrows and looked at her husband who pressed his lips together.

Ted Barrett's brother, Bill, ran this store. Duncan went to Bill's wife and asked her to help Dora Grace find a pair of pants to wear, and a simple but pretty dress. Then he thought again. "Ma'am, she…um, maybe…you know…" He held his hands over his stomach as he blushed. "Just maybe."

Bill's wife smiled. "If she wants pants, she'll grow out of them."

Duncan shrugged and handed his list to Bill who quickly filled his order. Then Duncan added three sticks of candy and a length of pretty ribbon when he saw what dress Dora Grace had chosen. He knew he had invited problems by allowing her to choose a dress, but maybe Dora Grace would convince Five Paws to stay and help. The Indian and Duncan worked well together, and Five Paws seemed to be capable of doing almost anything on the ranch.

As they left town, Duncan made one more stop at the post office to pick up his mail. There was a letter from Zadie. That single letter tugged at his soul. It wiggled and jiggled its way into his very core. As much as he didn't want to admit it, he was enjoying their correspondence. I wonder what nonsense she wrote this time?

3

Zadie met Ole Bill on Sunday afternoon and, as promised, he had his rowboat. He had already leaned the ladder against the tree. Getting into the boat shook her confidence, as it rocked back and forth, and she was certain it would turn over with her in it. "Please don't dump me in this water. There are snakes and only God knows what other creatures."

Ole Bill guffawed, making a deep rich sound. "I ain't gonna lets yous fall in. Now yous sits real quiet."

She gripped the sides of the boat and held on for dear life. The scent of the water and the swamp through which the river slowly flowed was sickeningly strong. There was no way she was going to move a muscle, but her stomach was doing somersaults until she arrived at the other side of the Blackwater River and stood on the patch of somewhat dry land.

With her small sketchpad in her pocket and two pencils poked through her dark bun, she reached between her legs for the hem of the back of her skirt. Gathering the material in her hand, she drew the hem between her legs and up to her waistband where she tucked it in. All she had left to do was pray that no one noticed her going up the tree.

Ole Bill held the ladder and looked in a different direction as she made her way to the two, fairly parallel, lower branches. Stepping from the ladder to the lower branch was easy.

She gripped onto the branch that contained the nest and prayed the lower branch didn't move as she made her way out to the egret nest. But as she got closer to the nest, both branches seemed to move in alarmingly different directions. By then, she was well over the water below. Don't look down. Don't think about it.

The nest didn't look that big from the ground, but it was about two feet across and probably a foot deep. She had to stand on her tiptoes to see into the nest, and the branch she was standing on gently swayed with every movement she made. She decided it was not safe to stay in the tree and sketch the nest. Instead, she had to memorize everything about it. Thicker longer branches made a platform, and then the actual nest was loosely woven of smaller branches. The very center was cup-shaped and lined with bits of moss and lichen. Three eggs appeared to be about the size of chicken's eggs, and they were a very pale bluish-green. The egret she had scared away, as she climbed the ladder, began to raise a fuss. It was time to leave.

Slowly, she eased away from the nest. Walking on one branch and holding onto the other seemed safe enough, until she heard one of them make a cracking sound, sending her heart into her throat.

"Miz Larkford, yous better gets out of dat tree."

As she put a foot on the ladder, the limb made another cracking sound. She couldn't seem to grab the ladder fast enough before beginning her descent. When she was eight, she would have shimmied her way out to the nest and back to the ladder. But she was no longer that adventurous. And by the time she was on solid earth, she was almost shaking.

"Did you hear that horrible noise? I feared the limb might break away."

Ole Bill nodded. "I's thinkin' yous gonna goes swimmin' in dat river. And dat big snake gonna swaller yous whole."

He's jesting…. Trying to scare me. I'm not going to fall for his nonsense. "I want to go back to the other side."

Again she held tightly to the sides of the little rowboat and peered at the water.

"Dere's a big monster snake that can open his mouth and eat my entire boat in one gulp. Yessiree. Hes sures can."

"Stop that, Ole Bill. There is no such snake."

"Den whys yous lookin' dat hard for him?" Ole Bill guffawed.

Once secure on the other side, she handed the man several small coins along with a silver dollar. He was most grateful. She also realized she was paying him not to tell her father. That made her wonder how many secrets he kept for the various townsfolk. Probably more than Poppa.

After she climbed up the bank from the river, she sat on the grass and sketched the nest while everything was still fresh in her mind. The nest itself looked as though the first wind would send it to the ground, yet she knew birds were expert weavers.

She had accomplished one goal, and she had one more on her list. She wanted to find that letter from Duncan Lorde that he'd written to her father. The letter had to be in her father's desk.

***

Duncan sat at his kitchen table and read the letter from Zadie. He laughed. She was toying with him, and he could play along. He

E. Ayers

pulled out his pen set and some paper.

My Dear Zadie,

I'm pleased to know that you can ride. We don't have foxhunts, but I'm sure your skills will come in handy when we have wolf hunts. As for the golf, the gophers don't appreciate getting whacked on the head by small, hard balls falling into their homes. When it comes to tea parties and dinner parties, you are most welcome to indulge in such frivolities. I can't imagine whom you could invite, but I wouldn't want to miss such a social event. As for how you spend your spare time, I'm sure you will find something that needs to be done. If you can't, you may ask me, and I will help you fill those rare moments. Twelve babies is a rather impressive number. I'm sure I will enjoy helping you towards that goal. But are you certain you want that many children? I would think your spare time would be greatly reduced in such circumstances.

Our weather varies in the winter. Some years we only have a few inches of snow, yet others have yielded snow deep enough to bury cattle in the fields. I promise you, it's very cold. When winter comes, providing you with so many children might be easily accomplished.

With love,

Duncan

He folded the letter and placed it in an envelope. He'd take it to town the next time he went. Tea parties and foxhunts, I doubt you've ever been on a foxhunt. Tallyho, my dear Zadie! You've plenty to learn.

***

E. Ayers

Zadie took advantage of the following afternoon to clean her father's office. It wasn't unusual for her to help by organizing his papers. No one in the house would think twice of her sitting at his desk. She filed quite a few records and searched for the letter from Duncan. Almost ready to give up, she found the note and pocketed it. When she finished dusting the room, she cleaned his oil lamp, trimmed the wick, and added more kerosene before heading to her bedroom.

Her hands shook with her excitement as she sat at her desk and pulled the letter from her pocket.

Dear Mr. Larkford,

I have some concerns about marriage to your daughter. I want her to be willing to come here and not coerced. But I'm worried that she's been accustomed to the finer things and will find life here tougher than what she is expecting.

My ranch is neither small nor large. I homesteaded and then purchased additional acreage from the railroad, and my ranch tends to be larger than most. I have excellent grassland and plenty of flatland for farming.

I never was keen on being on the water with my father and brothers, and as a result, I took a job on a farm outside of Edenton. I learned what I could about farming and tending animals during the time of my employment. When I discovered the opportunity here, I came west. My hard work is paying off. I do have additional income from my father's herring operations. It's a small percentage of the profit that is given to me, and the amount varies. That doesn't mean I'm wealthy, but it does give me more options than most ranchers around here.

We have Indians, but so far I've not had any problems. The Army keeps tabs on those who are off the reservation and works hard to keep the others on the reservation. In fact, I hired an Indian to help with branding this spring and I'm hoping that he stays here on the ranch and continues to help. There is another family in Creed's Crossing that has Indians living on their land and helping them.

My land extends to the road leading into Creed's Crossing, but it's an hour ride into town. That means I'm somewhat remote. I go to town every week to ten days for supplies and to check for mail. And although I do attend church occasionally, I'm often too busy to go weekly.

My days are long and hard. They start before the sun is up, and many times, I've tumbled into bed as the sun is setting. I need a woman who can work with me, be a partner, understand what I do, and not demand more than I can provide. I've heard of women who help to plow fields, but I can't imagine ever asking a woman to do such a thing.

I do hope she willingly takes over the kitchen garden. Last year, I could barely find the vegetables in all the weeds and grass, and if I found them, I wasn't certain how to cook them. I'm hoping for a better garden this year.

You asked about my success as a rancher. I have almost doubled my herd this spring. My bulls have been hand-selected. They seem to enjoy their work, and the cows have been willing and fruitful. I'm growing corn and wheat as insurance should we have a rough winter.

Zadie continued to read and found herself being drawn to the man on the other side of the Mississippi. He didn't boast, but he had a cocky attitude of a man who was confident, hard-working, and successful. But as she pondered some of what he wrote, she knew that his life was lonely and hers would be, too. Is this what I want?

She looked down at her hands. Every morning and night, she applied a salve of rosewater, glycerin, and beeswax to help protect them. And during the day, she often applied a special lotion that Abilene had made. It had helped with the redness. Her nails were now trimmed so that only a small line of white showed. It wasn't unusual for her to stain her nails and cuticles with paint, but her hands no longer looked like a lady's. Would it matter that her hands looked as though they belonged to a maid? From what Duncan had written, there was no one around to see her hands.

No one around - the thought echoed in her head. No Catherine to visit, no Abilene, no Mother or Father, no Ethel Kern to make clothes. Alone. Duncan is alone. No wonder he wants a bride.

With sadness, Zadie folded the letter and placed it in her pocket. With luck, she could return it to her father's desk before he discovered it was missing.

***

Duncan rode around the edges of his fields. The only things growing in his kitchen garden were weeds, and the little bit of corn that had sprouted now looked yellow and wilted. His wheat was fighting for survival.

His animals all congregated around the stream. They only wandered away long enough to look for grass or to nap under a tree.

Duncan headed for the Indian encampment and found his friend, Five Paws. Duncan waved a greeting and Five Paws came to him.

"We leave in few days. No rain. Our crops not come."

Duncan slipped off Rocky but held his reins. "Walk over here. I want to talk."

Together they walked a fair distance from the camp. Only when Duncan was certain his words would not be overheard, did he speak. "I want you to stay. You are my friend and a great help to me. I can pay you and keep you fed. Let your tribe go, but stay with me."

"Live like White man?"

Duncan nodded.

"We build house?"

Duncan swallowed the apprehension that rose in his throat. "We can do that."

Five Paws narrowed his eyes and slowly turned away. He stopped and looked back at Duncan. "I talk to Dora Grace."

Five Paws walked a few steps away.

Worry smacked Duncan in the gut. "You are my friend, and I need you."

***

"Zadie, I want to see you in my office."

Zadie cringed at her father's request. For some reason, he still looked at her as though she were a wayward child who needed direction. All she wanted was a cool bath and a chance to relax with her sketchpad. The last thing she wanted was a lecture from her father.

"Yes, sir, I'm coming." She entered his office and took the chair closest to the open window where a slight breeze stirred the curtains. Books sat on open shelves and everything else sat in plain cabinets with glass fronts. The cabinets matched his large, austere desk. Even the hooked rug on the floor was somber, in beiges, browns, and black. Her heart fluttered in her chest as she awaited her reprimand for whatever infraction he had discovered.

"You've been helping Abilene for several weeks now. How do you feel about your new chores?"

If this were a poker game, she feared she'd lose. She chose her words carefully. "I never realized how hard Abilene worked or what it took to keep this house running efficiently."

"Yes. She works very hard." Her father tapped the fingers of his right hand on the desk's blotter. "But have you learned how to do it without help?"

"Yes, sir." Please let me quit. I'm tired of

doing it.

"I'm glad to hear it." He continued his tapping. "Do you think you can run a household for a family?"

Her breath hitched. "You mean be a maid for a family? Have you hired me out?"

"No, my darling daughter. Will you be able to care for your own family one day?"

The chill that had seized her, evaporated. "Yes. For my own family, I can do it. For then it will be a labor of love."

He withdrew an invoice from his desk drawer. "And what is this?"

She started to take the paper, but when she saw whom it was from, she sat back and smiled. "If you insist on sending me to Mr. Lorde, I must be prepared. I have several more outfits coming, but Ethel will not have the wool until the end of August."

"Then you are preparing for your

journey?"

Duncan's letter to her father flew through her mind. "Yes, sir. I believe he's a good man, and I'm trying hard to become accustomed to the idea of marrying a man I barely know."

"The apple doesn't fall far from the tree. His father is a fine man, and he's raised his boys to be good businessmen. Any son of my good friend is not going to fail. Why that young man wants a ranch is beyond me, but if anyone can make a success of ranching, Duncan Lorde will be the man to do it."

Zadie wanted to have the same faith as her father, but the Lorde family was unknown to her. Furthermore, the few letters from Duncan Lorde had neglected to tell her very much, except that he could compose a decent letter and his penmanship was excellent. There had never been a drop or splatter of ink on the page, and no words had been crossed through. Naturally he'd want to show his best hand, and each page was exceptionally clean.

The following morning, Zadie sat on the side porch of the house and began to paint the egrets. She figured if she could capture her childhood habitat, she wouldn't be as homesick in a far-away land. She had dozens of sketches, and she wanted to be certain she had as many memories as possible put to canvas before she left Virginia.

For this painting, she'd chosen a large canvas and stretched it over a frame that had been made to hold it. She could imagine this painting above the mantel in her new home. The pristine white of the egrets made a nice contrast against the lush green of the trees and the green-black of the shaded water where the birds fished for food.

She wasn't alone very long before her mother joined her.

"How are you doing, my sweet daughter?"

"Fine."

"Your father seems pleased that you are making the adjustments needed to move west."

"Momma, I'll be fine, but I do worry about what sort of a man he might be. I still know almost nothing about him."

Zadie's mom smiled. "It is up to you to make a good man out of him. How you treat him will make all the difference. Take care of him, and he will do the same for you."

"But not every man is nice to his wife. I will not be abused."

"I doubt you will have to worry about that. He's been raised with good moral standards."

"I hope you are right, Momma. I've heard many stories about the west and how it is filled with saloons, gun slingers, and..." She lowered her voice. "Whores."

"If he wanted one of those, I'm certain he

would have found one. He asked for a good woman."

"And what if I am not good enough?"

"Any man would feel most fortunate to have you."

Zadie sighed. "I hope you are right."

A sound at the door made them both turn and look as Abilene brought them each a glass of iced sweet tea.

"I thought you ladies might like a little treat. I brought a plate of orange-ginger cookies to go with your tea." Abilene placed the tray on a small table near where Zadie and her mother were sitting. Then leaned over Zadie's shoulder. "Oh, I know that exact spot on the Blackwater River. It's just down the road. You do beautiful artwork. It looks as though you are staring right at the river."

"Thank you, Abilene. I'm painting this for my future parlor so I will always have a clear memory of Franklin and the water. It will warm my heart and keep me from being homesick once I've left."

Abilene tsked. "You don't need a painting. It's what's in your heart that counts. Once you move, your heart will belong to your husband and your home there. You'll be sending sketches home so you can share your new life with us."

"Here is my family. I wondered where everyone was." Zadie's father said, as he entered the porch. "Abilene, I hope you have more of that sweet tea for me."

The woman never answered. She merely left for the kitchen. She wasn't the type of woman to converse when she had work to do, and she needed to bring the man his tea.

"For you, my daughter." He passed her a letter.

She took the note and thanked him.

"Aren't you going to open it?"

"I'll read it later. I've been visiting with Momma. I don't want to be rude."

"Yes, but it is from your young man. I would think you'd be thrilled at receiving a letter from him."

"Oh, I am. But if you noticed, it is addressed to me and not to the entire family." She batted her eyes and rolled her bottom lip out for her father.

He laughed and kissed his wife's cheek before taking a rocking chair. "I swear that hill is growing steeper every day. Makes me feel like an old man."

Torn between painting and reading Duncan's letter, Zadie decided to paint. She listened to her parents' banter as she worked on the picture. It was obvious that her parents were very much in love. Certainly, if her parents could find that much happiness in an arranged marriage, she could too.

The first chance Zadie had, she stole away to her room and opened Duncan's letter. She couldn't stop blushing as she read his words. Oh my...

But somehow, she could feel herself being drawn to this man with a bawdy sense of humor. It wasn't overly suggestive or terribly salacious, but it was there, subtly tucked in his words.

***

Duncan was thrilled when he saw Five Paws and Dora Grace riding towards him. He raised his hand in a wave and Five Paws returned the gesture. They came with only a small bundle, and Duncan knew that meant he was expected to provide shelter. He had the extra room in the house, or they could use the barn. He worried about them having lanterns in the barn, and knowing Dora Grace, she'd think nothing of starting a fire for cooking in there. So he made a snap decision.

"Follow me." He took them to his house. "This room will be yours." He opened the door to the second bedroom that was totally empty. "And Dora Grace may use my stove. I will teach her to use it."

It didn't take much to restart the fire, as the embers from breakfast were still glowing. Dora Grace loved the water pump and quickly learned how to feed the stove with wood, but she didn't quite understand how hot the stove became until she burned her fingertips. With the stove hot, he let her make dinner even though he wasn't that hungry. Five Paws and Dora Grace devoured the meal and profusely thanked Duncan.

He left the cabin with Five Paws. Working

next to the Indian made the work go twice as fast, and they managed to accomplish more than expected. It was still late when they returned to the barn. The stalls had been swept and the barn was tidier than it had been in months. Dora Grace must have done that. On the cabin's porch railing were four of his shirts drying. As Duncan opened the front door of his cabin, he could smell cornbread and something else. Fruit?

It bothered him that there seemed to be little verbal expression between Dora Grace and Five Paws, as though everything was expected. There were no smiles, no outwards signs of joy. There was also no coffee, only a tea made from grass.

Duncan fixed a pot of coffee and let it brew as he ate his dinner. Since he only had two chairs, he brought a piece of log in that they could use. But both Five Paws and Dora

Grace sat on the floor.

Duncan wasn't certain what the cooked berries were because he didn't recognize them, but they were tart enough to curl his tongue. He added sugar and a sprinkle of cinnamon, but decided that he needed more sugar and something other than cinnamon. He was about to ask the Indians if they wanted some sugar but realized they were eating the berries without any problem.

Oh yes, there are differences. And it's going to take time. "I guess it will be the same with a wife."

"Did you say something?" Five Paws asked.

"Sorry. I was thinking about a wife and the many changes coming. It takes time to get used to another person, does it not?"

Five Paws laughed. "I went from mother who take care of me to wife not ready for me."

"How did you manage?"

E. Ayers

"At first, I was angry, but mother tell me be nice. Treat her like a newborn pup. Mother say Dora Grace learn. She learn quick."

"No one prepared her for marriage?"

He shook his head. "She afraid of me. Afraid of being with a man." He looked away. "It took many moons before she ready for baby."

Duncan gulped. He was certain that he understood. And that's not what he wanted to hear. Maybe he assumed that a woman would always want to be with him and sleep in his bed. Maybe the feelings a man had were not the same as the feelings a woman had.

-4-

Duncan soon discovered that having Dora Grace doing the cooking and Five Paws helping in the fields also meant he had little privacy. He often retired to the porch and stared into the waning light. Since Five Paws and Dora Grace were sharing the cabin, there was a need to add onto his little house before Zadie arrived. Every time he sketched a possibility, he tossed it aside. Zadie would want a real house and not a primitive log building that was only a few feet from the barn. He wrote to his father and asked for several house plans from which to choose. He hadn't seen any that he thought were suitable for a ranch. Most looked as though they belonged in the city, and they didn't seem practical or very functional for life in the west.

But there was one more letter he needed to write and this one wouldn't be easy. He sat on his porch with a lantern for light and began to write.

Dearest Zadie,

I have been informed that you are making an effort to learn new skills so that you are better prepared. I realize that I, too, need to make some changes. I've asked my father for some house plans, as I believe my cabin might not be to your satisfaction. I will also ask you if there is a house that you might desire. Brick is not available here. The house must be simple and not terribly ornate. I do not have time to cut fancy doodads. Plain is important. Also, you might want to pick out a stove for the kitchen. If you send your ideas for these things to me, I will do my best to provide them for you.

It has also crossed my mind that you might fear being with a man. Maybe men and women do not share the same feelings. I could sing my own praises, but that will tell you little. Anything I say about myself means nothing. I will tell you that I promise to treat you well and to love and cherish you as my father has my mother.

As you probably know, I am the fifth child and last son out of nine children. I do own a share of my father's business, and I receive a small amount of money each month. But it is only enough to supplement an income. If I stayed in Edenton, I would have bought a boat and worked beside my father catching herring. But I like land better than water. The ranch will give me my own income.

It is my understanding that you are an artist. I think you will find Wyoming to be beautiful.

He continued to work on the letter, hoping that she might open her heart to him.

***

Zadie painted or sketched every chance she had. Then one afternoon, she put her paints to one side and walked to where her friend Catherine lived. Visiting, uninvited, was not proper, but taking an offering of her orange-ginger cookies was a wonderful way to bypass protocol. The Duke house was plain. The simple porch was unadorned, and the windows were no different, with a single pane over a single pane. A swing hung from the ceiling of the front porch. Paint peeled in places, and two shutters needed repair.

She remembered while she was away at school, her mother writing with the news that Mr. Duke had been seriously injured. But as Zadie approached the front door, she wondered why the son had not made an effort to maintain the house for his parents. The brass doorknocker was in need of polish and from within she could hear Catherine scolding the twins. Sucking in a breath, Zadie knocked on the door.

Catherine opened the door. "Zadie, what brings you here?"

She passed the cookies to her friend. "I made them and I thought you might like to try them. I certainly wouldn't want to poison my soon-to-be-husband with untested cookies."

Catherine grimaced. "Give me a moment." Time seemed to tick by forever until Catherine returned to the door. "Please come in. I'll make tea for us."

The inside of the house was even plainer. Zadie followed Catherine into the parlor, past furniture that had seen better days

Mrs. Duke smiled as she entered the room. "Zadie, it's wonderful to see you. Catherine said you had returned."

"Yes, it's been awhile since I finished my schooling. Now I'm learning to do the domestic things that I've always taken for granted."

"I don't understand. I thought your family had a maid. Did she leave?"

Zadie put her hand to her chest. "Abilene would never leave. She raised my father. We couldn't imagine life without her. We all love her dearly."

Mrs. Duke raised her eyebrows. "You have no idea how lucky you are. After the war, my momma had to do everything."

There was something in Mrs. Duke's voice that Zadie didn't like.

Mr. Duke called to his wife, and Mrs. Duke excused herself.

Catherine appeared with a pot of tea and three cups. "I'm sorry to keep you waiting. Your cookies look delicious."

Zadie laughed. "Thank you. I wish everything I baked were as good. My biscuits could be used as weapons or maybe ship's ballast."

Catherine laughed as she poured the tea. "I doubt that."

Zadie rolled her eyes. "At least, my pies are good."

"Tell me about your man."

Zadie shrugged. "We are corresponding.

I can tell he has a wonderful sense of humor, and he seems to be making a success at ranching."

Catherine nibbled at a cookie. "Oh, these are good."

"Thank you." Zadie looked at the doorway. Satisfied there was no one to hear her words, she then returned her gaze to her friend. "I wanted to ask you if you'd like to bring the children to our house one day. I'd like to make some sketches of them. Consider it a gift for your anniversary or new home."

Catherine put a finger to her lips, and then whispered, "I hate it here."

"We can talk more when you bring the children. Do they each have a favorite toy? If so bring them. Dress them casually. I want them comfortable when they sit for me."

Again, Catherine whispered, "It's impossible to make children vanish as though they don't exist. Yet I am expected to work like a dog without any thanks." She stopped for a moment and looked towards the doorway. "John's parents want me to do everything, but they also want the children to stay out of sight and be perfectly quiet." She frowned. "It's impossible."

Zadie nodded and finished her tea. "What day may I expect you?"

"I will try to sneak away on Saturday, otherwise it will be Sunday."

"Wonderful. I look forward to our visit and to seeing the children." Zadie gave her friend a hug and left the house. Her heart was heavy as she walked home. She wanted to talk to Catherine about marriage, but there was a pall in that house that Zadie didn't dare attempt to breach.

On Sunday, Zadie returned from church and found her friend waiting for her. Both of the children had been dressed in their very best clothes, yet they both looked disheveled, and they were fighting.

Abilene took over and occupied the children in the kitchen while the adults ate their noon meal. Then Zadie's father took the twins outside and let them play on the swing in the backyard.

By the time Zadie was ready to sketch the children, they were sweaty and cantankerous. After positioning the children on the porch swing in such a way that they weren't even looking at each other, Zadie sketched them, ignoring the dirt and wrinkles in their clothing. Using her chalks, she made notes on skin colors and hair colors. The twins were alike, but in a way, they weren't.

While Abilene brought lemonade for everyone to drink, Zadie spent time sketching the twins sitting apart from each other. Satisfied, she turned the children loose and let them play in the yard. "Oh, Catherine, how do you do it every day?"

"By the end of the day, I'm a total wreck. John and I have fought so many times because he thinks it should be easy for me. It's not."

"Doesn't John help?"

"No. Raising children is a woman's job."

"But what about his parents' home? Forgive me, but it appears to need a few repairs."

"If he even attempts to do something, his father is bellowing at him. Last year, we simply gave up and decided if the house fell on top of them, so be it. We should know this week if we can buy the Baxley house. It's far enough away that my mother-in-law won't be visiting, because she doesn't dare leave her husband for more than a few minutes."

"What will they do with you gone?"

"I don't care. They have no right to mistreat

us. Let them pay for what they could have had for free, if they had only been kinder."

"Oh, Catherine. I can see how upset you are."

"I feel I cannot survive another month. In two weeks, if we do not have the house, I will pack my bags and leave for my parents' home. I'm no longer capable of withstanding this constant mistreatment from his parents."

Squeals of laughter caught Zadie's attention. She watched the children who were now playing with the neighbor's dog. "I don't know who is having more fun, the twins or Princess."

Catherine laughed. "I'm not certain if my daughter knows that the dog is supposed to be fetching. Zadie, thank you for inviting me, my children need to run and play every day." She looked around as if she feared being overheard. "Instead, they are being forced into being quiet little mice. They have too much energy to be silent all day long for John's parents. His parents even complain about their footfalls on the floors."

Zadie wanted to ask her friend all sorts of questions about marriage, but maybe Catherine wasn't the person to answer. Catherine had once been a beautiful golden blonde with blue eyes that sparkled. Now the sparkle was gone, and she looked like a raccoon with tired circles around both eyes. She appeared to be ten years older and her hands were red and raw. When Catherine left, Zadie realized she now had more questions than ever.

Monday, Zadie's dad huffed as he walked into the house. "That hill is killing me. I'm going to have to start taking the horse when I go downtown." He settled into his office and called Abilene. "Bring me some sweet tea. A big glass. Lots of ice."

"Poppa, are you all right? You are very red in the face."

"I'm fine, my darling Zadie. I think my years are catching up to me and this heat isn't helping." He pointed to the chair. "Come join me and tell me about your day."

She couldn't stop the single giggle that slipped for a second from her throat. "I made bread. There were still a few dried apple chips from last year, and I broke them into small pieces. I made cinnamon-swirl bread, but instead of adding raisins, I used those pieces of apple chips. Abilene said I need to experiment because I don't know what I will have available to me once I move away." She looked at Abilene entering the room. "She's taught me to make blueberry muffins and explained how easy it is to use other fruit. I also found a few ripe peaches on the tree in the backyard. I took them and made a peach pie. We can have that tonight for dessert."

"Ah, she's doing a fine job in the kitchen," Abilene said as she placed a tall glass in front of the man she had raised.

He patted his generous girth. "If my daughter keeps baking all those delicious things, I'll have to buy new clothes. I do hope that young man of hers appreciates a good meal." He took a sip of the tea and then reached in his coat pocket. "Here's another letter for you."

Zadie's breath hitched as she took the envelope. "Excuse, me. I want to return to my painting."

As she stepped outside, she heard her father say, "You only want to read that letter where no one will see you blush."

She giggled as she opened the note, then called back to her dad, "He doesn't write such things." Well, maybe.

Quickly, she read through the letter and knew she'd reread it several times until she had absorbed everything. This one was serious as he wrote about his life, his family, and living in the west. He had enclosed several tidy sketches of floor plans for a house. She looked at them, and then continued to read.

Since I don't have a picture of myself to send to you, I figured I could show off my artistic skills and draw my image for you. This is Rocky and I. I hope you know which is which.

Zadie grinned as she looked at his sketch. Oh, Duncan, you look a little long in the face, and I didn't realize that living in the west would cause your hair to grow so far down your neck. I'll have to ask him if Rocky has a frown or a mustache. She folded his letter and returned it to the envelope. You are asking for it this time. Just how ugly can I make myself? You're going to think twice before accepting me as a bride.

***

Duncan had two letters from Zadie and another from his father waiting for him at the post office in town. Now in the quiet of the evening, he opened the one from home. There were only a few lines from his father and the rest of the envelope was filled with house plans.

The letters from Zadie were dated and he started reading her first one. She had responded more seriously and also sent house plans that had been taken from a magazine. Two were outrageous and he snickered as he looked at them. One he was certain must have been an English mansion, the other probably belonged to a lumber baron or some other wealthy person, but the third one had some possibilities and looked very much like one his father had sent. He wasn't certain, but he thought he'd seen a plan for something very similar at Barrett's store. It was a little bigger than he wanted to build, and he wouldn't have access to the tiles for roofing, nor did he know if tiles would survive the cold winters. He could mimic the shape and use a standing seam roof.

But he wanted to build a log house. They were warmer in the winter than the houses that depended on large coal stoves to heat them. He kept envisioning a two-story home with a big wrap porch. He was running out of time. If he was going to have a house ready for her, he needed to start it tomorrow.

The second letter was brief. She wrote

mostly about her new domestic skills. And when she described some of the breads and cookies, he thought he might die from hunger before she came.

But when he opened her sketched portrait, his heart stopped.

***

Zadie's dad had relieved her of the household chores, but Zadie found herself doing things to help Abilene. By midday, it was too hot to work, and Zadie often spent her afternoons on the side porch. If there was going to be a breeze, even a hot one, the side porch always caught it. Her mother and Abilene often joined her as she painted.

Abilene would sit in such a way that she could keep one foot on a treadle that worked an overhead fan. Zadie wasn't certain what

E. Ayers

Abilene was crocheting with such tiny cotton thread, but whatever it was, it was growing daily. Zadie's mom often read. And Zadie worked on several paintings. The egret picture was almost done, as was the still life of the peonies that were in her mother's favorite vase. And she had completed several watercolors of the flowers that bloomed throughout Franklin and the various fruits as they came into season. She figured she could decorate the bedrooms and her dining room with the cheerful watercolors.

A knock on the front door sent Abilene scurrying to answer it. The heat of summer had kept her father home in the afternoons, unless he absolutely had to see a patient. But it wasn't unusual for one to come to him.

A few minutes later, Zadie could hear her father and another man laughing. The sound of her father's laughter rolled over her, bringing flashes of pleasant childhood memories. "I have a feeling that whoever came is a friend and not a patient."

"I believe you are right," Zadie's mom answered. "I haven't heard him laugh like that in years."

"I've worried about Poppa. I've never seen the heat get to him as it has this summer."

"He's fine. We're getting older, and he's no longer that invincible young man I married." Her knitting needles clicked nonstop as she spoke. "He's always believed in being careful, and he washes his hands and everything around him all the time. I think he's been extra careful as he's aged."

"Oh, you and Poppa are not old. Did you not say that Abilene raised Poppa? She must be twice as old and look at her energy."

"Hardly twice as old. She was in her early teens when your father was born and she refused to leave when the war ended. And yes, she's spry for her age. I know she's enjoyed teaching you this summer and having your help."

"You should have had me learn sooner."

"But you would have complained bitterly if we had--"

"Zadie, come here," her father called. "I want you to meet someone."

She glanced at her mother as a feeling of horror raced through her. Quickly she wiped her hands on her paint cloth and attempted to untie her paint frock that covered her old faded green and white day dress as she made her way to her father's office.

She had managed to undo the top portion of the frock so that it folded over the skirted portion and at least hid some of the paint splatters. "Yes, Poppa."

"Come in, my darling daughter, and meet

your future father-in-law. This is Reginald Lorde. Reginald, my daughter, Zadie."

Her vocabulary escaped, along with every sensibility. By sheer rote, she managed to offer the man her hand.

"I'm pleased to meet you, Zadie. I certainly would never have recognized you from your picture." Reginald Lorde was a fine-looking man for his age and impeccably dressed. His skin was weathered, his eyes were hazel, and his hair was an ash blond with slight curl.

"M-m-my picture?"

"Zadie, please sit," her father ordered, as he pointed to a chair situated near his desk.

She sat and waited, certain that she knew what was coming. The tingle up her spine ended with a series of stabs someplace behind her eyes and a fog threatened to whisk her away.

"Why did you send this to Duncan?"

She gazed at the drawing she had made of the chinless, big-eared woman. Bucked-toothed and extremely snubbed nosed, with beady eyes, the image appeared to be of a woman who was older than dirt. Then she shifted her gaze to her father before settling on Mr. Reginald Lorde. She couldn't hold back the giggles that bubbled from her. "It was a joke."

Mr. Lorde stood, came to her, and took her hand. "Miss Larkford, my son knew your drawing was a joke, but he was very concerned about your willingness to marry him. He doesn't want you forced into a marriage where you will be unhappy."

***

Duncan chose the spot for the house. It was slightly southwest of the barn and the cabin, but not too far. He knew what it was to run from the barn to the house in a downpour, or worse, to trudge through snow. Plus, he didn't want to drop another well or buy another windmill. He turned the house so that it backed up to the barn and it faced the road to Creed's Crossing. It would be the first thing anyone would see when visiting. He calculated the size of the rooms, and then created a foundation.

He and Five Paws worked on the house almost nonstop, but Duncan's heart was not in it. Zadie's clipped retort and her picture left him wondering. He was positive it was all a joke. But what if she really didn't want to come and her parents were forcing her? He couldn't shake that feeling.

He and Five Paws hefted a log into place. "Do any of your people ever marry because they are told to marry someone?"

"Yes. It happen."

"Is the couple happy together?"

Five Paws shrugged. "Many time, she not very happy."

"I want Zadie to be happy."

"You always write words to her. That not make her happy?"

"I don't know."

They put several more logs into place before Duncan said more. "I sent my father the money for Zadie to come out here, but I also told him I didn't want her to come unless she was willing. I worry her father is forcing her into marrying me."

"In our tribe, women given to men... I do not know your words. Big men."

"Status, high rank, honor, importance..."

Five Paws grabbed another log and Duncan picked up his end. He didn't want to let on that his arms and shoulders were burning with each lift. They were already working above their heads and using ladders to put the logs in place.

The large squared logs fit tightly together and didn't need the chinking of rounded logs. But it was similar to putting together a puzzle. Duncan was determined to have the house built and serviceable before Zadie came.

Dora Grace wasn't exactly the best cook, but her meals were better than what he'd been able to prepare for himself. The foods were plain and often lacked flavor or were too salty. He satisfied himself with the fact that he didn't have to cook. And after working with logs all day, he only wanted to eat and crawl into his bed.

On Friday, he took the day off, and they all went to town. Dora Grace wore her dress, and they took the buckboard. She sat up straight and acted very proud.

Duncan needed more nails, and with

luck, there would be letters waiting for him. But he almost didn't care. His arms ached to the point that holding the reins was an effort.

Maybe Zadie wasn't the woman for him. Highly educated and from a well-to-do family, she seemed like a good match for him based on their backgrounds. But maybe there was a reason that she had not yet married. Most women he knew were swept off their feet as soon as they were old enough to marry. Not Zadie. From what his father had told him, she was the one turning down suitors. Maybe she didn't want to marry. He'd heard there were women who didn't want a man or to have a family.

When he'd lived at home, he'd had young women following him around and vying for a chance to be with him. He hadn't been ready to marry. He wanted more out of life. Now he had his own life, and his dreams were within his grasp. Was she the same? Was she looking for more, too?

There were several letters awaiting him, and he opened his father's immediately. He scanned it and found the passage he wanted.

She's positively lovely. Dark hair and eyes like her father's. Her artwork is breathtaking. No one is forcing her to marry. From what I saw, she doesn't seem the least bit spoiled. She's quite open to the idea of marriage, but wants to get to know you, so don't expect to marry her the moment she sets foot in Wyoming. Give her a chance. I'm sure you will woo her without any problems.

That was all Duncan wanted to hear. The rest of his day went well. He couldn't wait until he was home and had some time to himself to read Zadie's letter.

It was late when Duncan sat on his

porch. The sun had vanished behind the western mountains. He lit a lantern and pulled Zadie's letter from his pocket.

By now you probably know that my hair is long and the darkest possible brown. I was surprised by the visit from your father. In fact, I felt awful. I was not dressed to receive visitors. Earlier in the day, I had been helping Abilene, our maid, and then was enjoying a very hot and sticky afternoon by painting on the porch.

He continued to read the rest of her letter. She sounded contrite, like a child who had been caught lying. He almost felt sorry for her, or maybe his feelings were also for his own loss since their games had come to an end. He had enjoyed their sparring.

I will leave here on August twenty-first. I'm sending some trunks ahead and I understand they will arrive in Creed's Crossing on August sixteenth. If you will take them to the house, I would appreciate it. They contain many of the things that I will need for our house and some clothes. Please bring Rocky when you meet me, otherwise I might not recognize you from your picture.

One last important item that you need to understand, I will not marry you until I am certain that we can be compatible. I refuse to be trapped in an unhappy marriage, or with a man who displeases me, or vice versa. I want us, if possible, to find love or at least a sensible companionship.

Zadie

He read the letter several times. Companionship was not what he wanted.

E. Ayers

Rocky was a companion. He wanted a woman who could warm him on cold nights. But even that wasn't enough. If they were to be yoked, he wanted a real partner. He knew he was ready for Zadie, but was she ready for him?

Part Two

5

Zadie opened her wardrobe and checked every shelf to be certain she'd not forgotten anything. Ethel had promised to ship several skirts and dresses to her, along with a heavy coat. The knowledge that she was leaving her childhood home for an unknown place to be with a man she'd never met offset the fun of a new wardrobe. Tears slipped down her cheeks. She felt that she might as well be moving to Africa, for the west was just as terrifying.

"Are your ready?" Abilene asked, as she brought a tray with iced sweet tea and lemon cookies into the bedroom.

"Yes and no. I am packed, but I will never be ready to leave you or my parents."

"You will be fine. You need to allow your heart to find love."

"I'm trying. But I have too many questions and concerns."

"You think too much."

"How will I know him when I see him? What are the odds that Duncan looks like his father, only younger?"

Abilene laughed. "How many men do you think are going to be waiting for you in Creed's Crossing? And after that portrait you sent him, how will he recognize you?"

Zadie fell into a round of giggles. It took work to force out her words. "He…will…know…I am…the opposite."

Abilene grinned. "That was very unfair of you. Were you afraid that he would want you only because you are pretty?"

Zadie shook her head as she attempted to compose herself. "I want him to want me because he cares about the person I am."

"Then be honest with him. And write home often. We will all miss you."

A few hours later, Zadie said one last set of goodbyes as she stepped onto the train. Traveling alone was considered improper, but she had refused her mother's plea to travel with a chaperone. I'm not a child, nor am I naïve when it comes to people. I can take care of myself. Her valise was filled with all sorts of fruits and cookies, along with a change of clothing, and some toiletries. But as she located her seat, her confidence waned.

I'm not going to cry. I'm not going to cry. But the tears kept welling in her eyes and she tried to push them away. Smile. But her lips refused to obey.

E. Ayers

The train's bell jangled and the whistle blew. She put her fingers to her lips and threw kisses to her family. Life as she knew it would never be the same. She dissolved into full-blown tears as the train pulled away from the station.

It was a while before she composed herself enough to realize she was not alone in the railroad car. Three other women sat together staring at Zadie as though she might eat them for dinner. She tried to smile. "I am Zadie Larkford, and I am going to Wyoming."

The women nodded before she quickly turned away.

Traveling alone was unthinkable in certain circles. Dressed in black and dove gray, she probably resembled a widow in mourning, and in theory, that should keep her safer from the type of men who preyed on virginal women. Furthermore, she knew these colors wouldn't show the dirt of train travel.

She turned to the window and stared at the fields and woods that lined the tracks.

She had ridden the train enough in her life to know how it jiggled on the tracks, the amount of dirt and soot that blew through the open windows, and the constant noise from the wheels. She pulled out her sketchpad and doodled. Her tickets were pinned in her pocket. She had memorized her entire trip and the various stations where she had to change trains.

She thought about the lovely going-away tea her mother had prepared for all of their friends. Everyone was thrilled for her, although a few worried about her moving to such a wild place. Catherine cried as she'd said goodbye, and Zadie tried to assure her friend that she would be fine. But as Zadie stared out the train window at the passing fields, she knew deep inside that her confidence about living in such primitive conditions was lacking.

The whole trip by rail went smoothly. Each time she changed trains, her tickets had given her a Pullman car, which was always comfortable. She was provided food, and when necessary, a sleeping area. Before she left the train for the last leg of her trip, she washed and changed into a fresh dress.

This dress was a charcoal gray with stripes of browns, greens, black, and tiny yellow flowers. She wanted to look her best, although she wasn't certain if her intent was to impress Duncan, or if it had to do with her own pride. She pulled her hair into a tight bun and pinned it. After checking her image in the mirror one more time, she packed her comb and other things into her valise.

She only had a few hours by stagecoach to Creed's Crossing. Picturing a lovely coach like the one her father had for family outings, she was shocked when a large, fat-bellied, wooden stagecoach awaited her arrival. A family sat on top of it and a Negro sat on the back of it. Inside, it was crowded and the stench of unwashed humans was enough to nauseate her. She sat between two women and tucked her valise between her feet. Whatever pity she had felt for the family riding on top, quickly vanished as she wished she could have joined them.

A woman who had painted her face asked where she was going.

"Creed's Crossing."

The woman chuckled. "You a mail order bride?"

"No."

"Oh, you ain't gonna admit it. Most of them don't. But you're prettier than most."

Zadie squared her shoulders. "My betrothed is the son of an old family friend. He moved out here a few years ago and established his ranch. Now he is ready for me. I'm not marrying a stranger."

"Humph!"

"Think what you want." Zadie hated the implication that she was a desperate female looking for a male. She didn't need to marry Duncan. She was free to return home at any time. Her father had given her sufficient money for return tickets if she felt as though she needed to come home.

The stage bumped, tossing her against the woman beside her.

"Why are you traveling alone?" the woman asked.

"I have no need of a chaperone."

The woman with the painted face laughed. "Too poor to pay the passage of a chaperone?"

Zadie had managed to get to Wyoming

with few questions. Now she felt as though she were being interrogated. The stage bounced and bounced some more. If it didn't bounce it shook. Never had she traveled at such speed in a stagecoach, and she feared it would rip apart, killing her before she reached Creed's Crossing.

Another woman eyed her for a moment and then commented, "Oh, she's mail ordered. All dressed up for her intended. Gonna run to the nearest preacher to be married."

Zadie had had enough. She rolled her eyes and dropped her gaze to her glove-covered hands. Already, the gloves were dirty and all she had done was get off the train and onto the stagecoach. She figured her face was just as filthy. The thought of being stuck inside this horrible means of transport grated on her already-frazzled state. *This is not the way I want to meet Duncan. Oh, why do I* care? Mail order bride? How absurd! Oh please take me off this coach.

***

Duncan rode into town with the buckboard. So far he'd brought home nine large crates and stacked them in the barn, unable to imagine what she might have sent ahead of her journey. But he figured with the buckboard, he was prepared for whatever else might be coming with her.

His skin prickled with anticipation and something in his gut knotted. Their letters back and forth only gave clues to the person that she was and nothing assured him of this match. Even his father's words didn't convince him. Life on his ranch was not the same as living in Edenton. Certainly Franklin, Virginia, isn't much different from Edenton.

He thought about his parents' home. It was a lovely older home that faced the water of the Albemarle Sound. His mother ran that household with an iron fist. There was a maid and a cook. His mom entertained all the right people, and was a matron of Edenton society. His father was respected as a businessman with several boats and a herring canning business. But Duncan and his siblings had grown up understanding hard work.

He pulled his mule to a stop in front of the dry goods store. There was nothing for him to do but wait. He paced up and down the street a dozen times. Ted Barrett gave him a cup of coffee. But nothing settled the feeling that grew inside of him. He went from minor doubts to a gut-wrenching feeling of panic.

The house was not ready. It was a shell with rooms that were unfinished. He was still awaiting the arrival of brick for the chimneys.

And if the bricks did not arrive soon, it would be too cold for him to build chimneys with mortar. It was a job that would have to wait until spring. Nothing was going according to plan, except his ranch. His herd was doing well, and he had harvested enough hay and wheat to last for several months if he needed it. His corn had barely survived the dry summer.

When he saw the dust far to the south of the town, he knew it was the stagecoach. How do I greet her? He should have thought through this situation before now, but he hadn't stopped long enough to consider what he should do. Now he only had a few minutes to decide.

His father's words to him flitted through his mind, as did that horrible drawing of her. What if she's not pretty? He knew he didn't care if she wasn't beautiful, but he expected her to be reasonably nice looking. He took a deep breath. The last four months of correspondence were over. He promised himself that it was her mind that had made him want her.

The stagecoach thundered into town and stopped. The driver called, "Creed's Crossing!"

It took a moment for the coach's door to open. A woman tossed out her valise and then stepped from the confines. The driver removed a small trunk from the rear and dropped it on the dirt road.

"Zadie?"

The woman his father had described looked up at him. "Duncan?"

Tears began to stream down her cheeks.

"Don't cry, sweetheart. It's over. Welcome to your new home." He wrapped his arms around her and she dissolved into tears.

"It was awful! Please take me home. I don't think I have the stamina to withstand another minute."

He helped her onto the bench of the buckboard. Then he picked up her trunk and valise and put them behind her. "Would you like to…use the…facilities or anything while you are in town?"

"Just take me far away from that stagecoach. That was horrid."

"I bought cookies and the most delicious sticky rolls. They are in that white paper."

She shook her head. "I'm too dirty to even think about eating. I want a bath and clean clothes."

He slapped the reins and his old mule, Nellie, took off towards home. The woman beside him was obviously worn out and distressed. He didn't know what to say.

At one point, she had called herself plain. She was anything but plain. Zadie Larkford was exquisite, with rich dark brown hair. She had long eyelashes over dark brown eyes and a cute little nose with a perfect little rosebud mouth. He couldn't have asked for a prettier woman. And under that fascinating exterior was a woman who was smart and funny.

Thoughts of her intelligence lingered in his mind until he turned them around and directed them at himself. His father didn't want him to go to college. Said it wasn't needed. A man needed to get a real job and make something of himself. College was for doctors and religious people. Beyond that, it was a waste of time and money. Oh, father, maybe someday you will understand that I don't like the water or the stench of fish. I don't want your life. I'm happier here.

He realized she was falling asleep, so he put his arm around her and tucked her to his side. Her eyes closed and they didn't flutter open. That was probably best, for he was not ready to explain an unfinished house. The balance of his life depended on how well he handled the next hour of his life. This was one time he didn't want to make a mistake.

***

Duncan reined his mule to a stop as soon as the house became visible. "Zadie, wake up. We're here."

She stirred and then righted herself in the seat. "Oh, I can't believe I fell asleep. How terribly rude of me. Please forgive me."

"I'd rather not. I--"

Wide-eyed she stared at him. "What do you mean that you won't forgive me?"

"I assumed that you were tired and comfortable in my presence. The combination allowed you to relax and trust me enough that you could sleep."

She glared at him. "And just where are we?"

"This is my ranch and that, up ahead, is the house." He sat a little straighter in the seat as he watched her looking around. His pride filled his chest and tugged at his cheeks.

He couldn't have picked a better time to view the house, as the sun was low in the western sky. The tin roof shimmered, but it wasn't the blinding reflection of the midday sun. He lightly slapped the reins and tsked at Nellie. They'd be there soon enough, and then he'd have to explain why the house wasn't quite finished.

"You wanted large. It will also be warm in the winter because of the construction. And if you look on top of the roof, you will see a cupola - I learned that from my father. Heat in the summer rises through it and out of the house. As soon as I had it in place, we could feel the difference in the house as we worked."

His puff of pride quickly faded, as he got closer to the house. Whatever self-esteem he had dissolved into a tangled web of pity in his guts. I need to just tell her and not shock her when she enters the place.

"Zadie, the house isn't finished. I have a cabin that I'm living in, and it was fine for me. But you wanted a real house and I understand. I've worked hard to build this for you, but it's not completed. When it's done, it'll be a real beauty."

"You built it?"

"Yes, with the help of Five Paws. I'm waiting on the man who does the plastering. He'll be here in another few weeks. Then it will look better. And my bricks for the chimney should be here next week." He grabbed a quick breath and kept going. "I'll have to bring the cattle down before it gets too cold so I probably won't have much time to build all the chimneys this fall. You'll get one. Then it will be too late to build the rest of them."

"What do you mean too late?"

"It gets too cold and the wet mortar freezes. It has to be warm for the mortar to set."

"Are you saying I can't live in the house?"

"Oh, it's more livable than my cabin was that first year. But you might not want to live in it."

"It's…it's large but primitive."

He pulled to a stop by the front door of the two-story log house with a two-story porch that surrounded it, and helped Zadie down.

As he set her on the ground in front of him, he realized how tall and willowy she was. The sound of a hammer told him that Five Paws was working someplace inside, probably on the stairs that would lead to the attic. They had cut the risers and treads two days ago. Then they spent yesterday trying to make certain everything was clean and neat.

He followed behind Zadie with his heart sitting in his throat. He couldn't stand her silence. Do you like it or not? Say something.

After wandering from room to room, she took the staircase to the second floor. A few steps down what would become the hallway, she stopped and screamed. Turning quickly, she almost knocked him off his feet as he caught her.

"What's wrong?"

Her face drained of color and she fainted. He held her in his arms and called for Five Paws. "Bring me some water. Be fast."

Seconds ticked by like minutes. He knew it was warm in the house, but he couldn't imagine it being warm enough to make a woman pass out. He tried to look around to see what might have frightened her. Oh, please don't be the kind of woman who is going to faint over a spider. She began to stir in his arms. Oh, please, where is the water? Hurry.

Five Paws returned with a full cup. Duncan lifted it to her lips and told her to drink. She did and her eyes fluttered open. Then she gasped.

"What is wrong?"

She pulled herself upright and stared at Five Paws. "I am so sorry. I was not expecting…an Indian." Her hands flew to her face. "Oh, and he's not dressed."

Duncan couldn't hold back his laughter. "What needs to be covered is covered. He is cooler than I am."

He wrapped his fingers around her slender wrists and pulled her hands from her face. "You'll get used to seeing him and his wife Dora Grace. Did you forget that I said they were helping me?"

She swallowed. "I did not forget, but I've never seen an Indian. I…didn't know…I'm sorry." She held out her hand. "I must have left my manners in Virginia. I am Zadie Larkford. Pleased to meet you, Mr. Paws."

Five Paws, with his thin-lipped, emotionless expression, looked at Duncan and then took Zadie's hand and turned it over as though she had something in it. When he realized there was nothing, he returned his gaze to Duncan.

Duncan smiled. "Like this." He took her hand and shook it. "Now you try."

Five Paws tried again, and from Zadie's expression, Duncan knew the man had held her hand too tightly. "Be gentle with her. She is not made of wood." Then Duncan turned his gaze to Zadie. "He doesn't have a first and last name, just a name. It is Five Paws."

"I can tell I have much to learn."

"Let me show you the rest of the ranch while we still have light."

She nodded. "Again, I am sorry, Mr.

Five Paws."

As Duncan and Zadie left the house, the sun was starting to dip behind the mountains setting the sky on fire with its burgundy, pink, and purple.

"You said it is beautiful here and you are right."

"Dora Grace will have supper ready for us." He took her to the cabin and opened the door.

Five Paws' wife greeted them with a big smile. Duncan knew she was excited and proud, for she was wearing her dress for this special occasion. The small cabin smelled of corned beef, potatoes, and cabbage. The aroma made his stomach growl in anticipation, even though that was what he'd told Dora Grace to fix for Zadie's arrival.

Duncan lit a lantern and introduced the two women. "Dora Grace doesn't speak much English, but she understands most of our words."

Zadie offered her hand and Dora Grace handed her a ladle. A chuckle broke loose from Duncan. He'd never thought to teach these Indians to shake hands. There was never a reason to do it.

Zadie looked at him and giggled. "I guess that didn't work quite as well as I was hoping."

He took the ladle from Zadie and handed it back to Dora Grace. Then pointed in one direction. "That is their room, and this is ours." He ushered her into his small bedroom. "If you wish me to heat the water for you, I will, but I'm assuming you might prefer the cool."

He handed her a cloth for washing and another for drying. "I think you will find whatever you need beside the ewer. After we've eaten, you may use the kitchen and fix a bath."

"And your lavatory?"

"We passed it on the way here."

"A privy?"

He nodded. "You will have running water in the house."

She heaved a breath and left the tiny bedroom that was barely large enough to hold the bed. When she returned, she walked past him with an expression that he couldn't quite decipher, but he decided she wasn't happy.

***

Zadie washed her face, hands, and arms. So far she wasn't thrilled with anything. She looked around the small room and wondered where she would sleep. She would never share a bed with him if they were not married. And he wasn't going to leave her alone in that unfinished house by herself, nor would she stay where Indians were sleeping in the next room.

Taking several deep breaths, she attempted to steady her quaking insides. I'm here, and I need to make an effort to adjust to this life. But that little ball of doubt rolled around inside of her and dented her confidence. She thought about the Paws who were living with Duncan and wondered. Certainly, he must trust them enough to allow them into his home. But all those horrid stories of how they attack the whites and cut the skin off their skulls... She shuddered at the thought. They don't look like wild beasts.

Content with being clean enough to eat, she left the room and found Five Paws sitting on the floor and two places set at the table. Duncan was pacing but stopped when he saw her.

"I washed up outside. Have a seat, unless you want to eat on the porch."

She shook her head. "This is fine."

He took her plate and placed two large

slices of corned beef on it along with some potatoes and cabbage.

"If that is for me, it is too much."

He looked at her and then at the plate. "I don't want you to be hungry."

She took his empty plate and fixed it for herself. "This is better. But where are they going to eat?"

Duncan raised his eyebrows. "It seems they don't like my chairs."

She turned her gaze to Five Paws who now had his wife sitting next to him on the floor. "We eat and then they eat?"

He nodded. "Dora Grace feeds me first."

"I have much to learn."

Duncan held a chair for her and seated her before taking his. He took the neatly rolled serviette and placed it in his lap, then offered a quick prayer of thanks. Zadie tried not to stare at him while she ate. He was handsome in an ordinary way. His light-brown hair had been sun bleached. His shirtsleeves were rolled, and his forearms and face were a golden bronze from the sun. His manners were impeccable even as he ate. He caught her stare and smiled as he chewed his corned beef.

The meal was plain but filling. When all the dishes were clean, she turned to him. "If you don't mind, I'd like to take a bath and remove the dirt from traveling."

Duncan grinned, showing off slight dimples. "Not a problem. Let me get the tub."

He walked out the back door and returned a moment later, carrying a large tub. "I keep two tubs on nails outside. The smaller one I use for laundry."

"Thank you." There was no way for her not to notice the strength in his arms and shoulders under his lightweight shirt as he hefted the heavy tub and placed it in the center of the small kitchen, which was nothing more than an alcove between the two bedrooms.

"I'll keep everyone outside until you tell me we can return."

"And where is my trunk that I brought with me?"

"I'll bring it in now."

A few minutes later, she found herself alone in the cabin. She heated some water and filled the tub. She didn't want a hot bath, just enough warmth to take the edge off the icy cold water that came out of the pump. She found her nightgown and robe. She looked at the water in the tub, and knew if she attempted to wash her hair in there, the water would be too dirty for a bath. She stripped to her chemise and unpinned her hair. She grabbed a pan and stood in front of the large sink.

Twice she washed her hair before the water ran clear. Then she twisted the length, wringing the water out of her locks until the twist formed a high bun. A few pins held it up and out of the way. Then she removed her chemise and stepped into the tub. It felt glorious after not being able to truly wash for days. It wasn't a real bathtub, but it was sufficient. "Maybe I'll adjust to this life. This isn't perfect, but it's not terrible."

She had to convince herself to seriously try to make this situation work. She continued to talk to herself in what resembled a whisper. "I will learn to love it."

A little pang of guilt needled her. She was keeping everyone outside and away from the house while she relaxed. She forced herself out of the water and dried off.

Wearing her nightgown and robe, she managed to empty the tub by bailing out the water and pouring the water from the small pan into the sink. It was a chore to empty the tub compared to pulling the plug on the porcelain tub back home. When she was done, she found her large lightweight shawl and wrapped it around her, hoping to give herself another layer so that she would remain properly covered in this most unusual situation. She let her hair down so that it might dry and then peered through the primitive curtain that covered the windows by the front porch before stepping out the door. Duncan was sitting on the steps.

"I'm sorry to have taken so long." She sat beside him.

"Don't be. Feeling better?"

"Oh, yes. Not quite like home but still relaxing."

He reached behind her and picked up one of her damp locks. "Your hair is longer than I imagined."

His forwardness didn't surprise her, but

the tingling that his touch elicited did. She sucked in her bottom lip, hoping to stop the feelings racing through her.

"You're very pretty. Why did you draw that horrible portrait?"

6

"I knew it. I knew you were going to ask me that."

Duncan looked with raised eyebrows at Zadie from where he sat next to her on the porch's steps. "Can you read my mind?"

"Not really. But I knew you would ask me eventually."

He dropped the strands of hair he held, leaned back, and put his elbows on the porch's floorboards. "So you've planned your answer?"

"Twenty times, and each story has been different."

"I don't want a story. I'd like the truth. Why?"

"Part of it was a joke. And part of it was a test to see if you would still like me if I were ugly." She stood and walked a few feet away. "I figured I must have really scared you, since you sent your father to our house."

"No. I caught your joke, and I already knew you were pretty. My father told me that it had been awhile since he'd seen you. He said you were a beautiful child with dark eyes and dark hair."

"I don't remember ever meeting him."

"He told me you were about ten or eleven at the time and seemed not the least bit interested in your father's visitor."

She nodded. "That's true. Poppa often had visitors. So why did you send your father?"

"I really did want to know that you were coming here willingly."

"I accepted the idea."

"But you are not happy."

She shrugged as she turned to look at him. "I would have preferred to stay close to my family. It would have been easier if you were in Courtland or Windsor. Even if you were as far away as Norfolk, Roanoke, or Richmond, Virginia…but here?" She stood, walked down the few steps before stretching her arms out in front of her and rolling her palms up. "I have no desire to be this far from my family."

"Then I will send you home. I don't want you to be here if you don't like it."

"No. I promised I would come and try." She came back and sat beside him. "For me, it's a matter of honor. I gave you my word that I would come. We need to know if we can make this work. That's why I said I would not marry you until I was certain."

She realized she was being drawn to him. Maybe it was his quiet demeanor and the fact that he was a gentleman. Maybe it was his looks. The resemblance to his father was apparent, but Duncan was lighter in coloring. There was nothing striking about him. He had a boyish face and a quick smile, yet there was something special. Confidence? Maybe. Whatever it was, she liked it.

Duncan stood and gave her his hand as he whistled. "That's to let Five Paws and Dora Grace know they can return to the cabin. They've been in the barn. Let's go to bed. Morning comes early here."

"Go to bed? I get the bed and you may sleep in the main room. You are not leaving me in a cabin with savages."

***

Duncan tossed a heavy wool blanket on the floor. This was not the arrangement he had pictured. Sleeping in the barn on hay would have been more comfortable. He wondered how Five Paws and Dora Grace endured sleeping on the floor all the time. But they also had animal pelts to cushion them.

He stared at the ceiling as bits of conversation flowed through his mind. How long would he be sleeping on the floor? He wasn't certain if he'd come to any conclusion as light from the rising sun streamed through the windows. He heard the sounds of others stirring and smelled coffee. He folded his blanket before placing it in the corner of the room. After checking the coffeepot, he fixed a cup and went outside.

The staccato of a hammer hitting nails emanated from the house. Five Paws had already begun working. Duncan followed the sound and found his friend nearing the top of the second-story staircase that led to the attic.

The banister for these steps could be installed at any time because this staircase would be enclosed as soon as the steps were finished.

Pride flowed through Duncan. He had completely designed the house and picked out the materials. It wasn't something from a set of plans by someone in New York or Chicago. This was all his from start to finish. He combined what he liked best from several sets of plans and redrew the house. He'd found the reddish wood in a large stand of trees by the stream that ran through his property and recognized it as being some sort of cedar from its color and scent. He'd taken those trees to a neighbor and had told him what he wanted. The neighbor had then cut them so that all fit tightly together. The rest of the wood had been ordered from the farm supply store. Now he was nearing the end.

When Five Paws drove the last nail,

Duncan smiled. "Ready to varnish the floors? With luck they will be dry and ready before the walls are plastered. It will save us time."

Five Paws nodded, but Duncan knew varnish meant nothing to his friend. Two hours later, they had started brushing the varnish onto the wooden floors. By the time they quit for a noon meal, both Duncan and Five Paws had a headache. Getting away from the house and the strong fumes from the varnish felt wonderful.

Duncan was halfway through his meal when he realized he'd not seen Zadie. He asked Dora Grace, but she indicated she did not know. His bedroom was empty, and the bed was made. Zadie must have wandered off. He needed to speak to her about that. It wasn't safe. She couldn't take off as she did when she lived in a town. He went outside and called to her, but there was no answer. Now he had floors to do and couldn't go looking for her. But a feeling of panic sliced through him like a cold knife. She probably wasn't far and he knew he was being overly protective. After his internal debate, he came to the conclusion that she was capable of taking care of herself. And if he went after her, it would make him appear to be controlling. She'd get back on that train tomorrow if she thought I was attempting to dominate her.

He returned to the house and worked on the floors. With two of them applying varnish, it didn't take long to coat the floors. They'd only stop long enough to retrieve another can of varnish. The raw wood floors soaked the liquid up faster than he had expected, and he feared running out before he had completed all the rooms. As they started on the kitchen, he heard a wagon pull up outside.

"Duncan? Are you in here?"

The voice belonged to Zadie and relief

washed over him. "Yes, in the kitchen. Don't come in. I'll come to you."

"You're varnishing. I can tell by the odor."

"What do you know about varnish?"

"What don't I know? I'm an artist."

"Oh. Will it ever stop sinking into the wood? I worry that I've not bought enough. I don't want to take time to go into town to buy more."

"Let me see." She stepped into the front room and looked into the parlor. "How long ago did you do this floor?"

He shook his head. "A few hours ago."

She walked to the staircase and lightly touched her finger to a tread. "This is almost dry. Leave at least a day between coats. The next coat should stay on top." She touched his forearm. "Do you have turpentine to remove what you didn't put on the floor? It looks as though you've done a fine job of varnishing your skin."

"I have some."

"You're going to need it."

"And where have you been?"

"I have no clue, but I had fun. I just rode around."

"I hope you didn't ride through my crops."

She rolled her eyes at him. "I'm not daft."

"Did you harness the mule?"

"Of course. It wasn't much different from my father's cart or the carriage."

"We need to talk before you do something like that again."

She turned on her heel and walked away from him. She drove to the small outbuilding where he parked the buckboard, while he tried to decipher if they had just had an argument. He wasn't certain what to call it. But he knew she wasn't about to take orders from anyone, including him. And that worried him more than her running off alone without any protection.

***

Zadie finished grooming the mule and went into the cabin. Dora Grace was hand sewing on some fuchsia material. Zadie politely said hello and went to the kitchen to wash in the sink. When she was satisfied that she was clean enough, she turned to Dora Grace. "When will the men return for supper? I'm willing to fix it."

Dora Grace smiled.

"Do you understand anything I say?"

Dora Grace smiled and put her sewing to one side. She added a few pieces of wood to the stove and started a pot of coffee.

Zadie let out a sigh and attempted to show with gestures what she had asked as though playing a parlor game.

Dora Grace watched her and smiled.

Zadie felt as though the dog, Princess, who lived next to her parents, understood more than Dora Grace. Zadie pressed her fingertips to her forehead. Oh, I'm being unfair. Didn't Duncan say that she understood but didn't always know enough to reply?

I give up. She went to the bedroom and retrieved her Conté sticks and her lap-sized drawing board. She took them to the porch because it seemed slightly cooler out there than it was in the house with a hot stove. Flipping through her sketchpad, she chose one scene. Abilene was right. I'll be drawing and sending pictures home to share with my family.

Dora Grace brought Zadie a cup of sweetened coffee. Deep inside, Zadie knew the young woman was trying. "Thank you, Dora Grace. This is very kind of you."

Dora Grace smiled. It was an odd smile that appeared to almost be a sneer, but Zadie knew from the woman's eyes that she was smiling.

Dora Grace pointed to what Zadie was

drawing.

Zadie nodded and then pointed to a spot for Dora Grace. "Please sit."

Dora Grace instantly sat.

Zadie shook her head. She took Dora Grace's hand and led her to the corner of the porch that held a lone chair. "Sit here."

Dora Grace tilted her head.

Zadie went to go back to where she was sitting and Dora Grace started to move. "No! Stay. Sit."

Dora Grace sat.

I'm talking to her as if she's a dog. I can't believe I'm doing that. I need her to smile. Zadie picked up her cup, took a sip, and smiled broadly at Dora Grace.

Dora Grace returned the smile and Zadie instantly began to sketch Dora Grace with the colorful Conté sticks. Twice Dora Grace tried to move and each time Zadie held up her hand. "No. Sit."

If Zadie smiled, so did Dora Grace.

Dora Grace's long dark hair had been pulled into two tails that were held in place with strips of leather, but strands had escaped, leaving long tendrils near her face. Her dark skin was a burnished red and her pretty white teeth added a strong contrast to her dark body.

Zadie would have said the woman's hair was black but when the sun caught it, it was a very dark brown with blue-black highlights like the Chinese people. Dora Grace's eyes were almond shaped and tilted upward giving her a pleasant countenance even when she wasn't smiling. Zadie decided that Dora Grace was very young but had no idea what her age was.

Taking a bit of cotton wrapped around a wooden stick, Zadie blended several areas and then smiled at what she had done. She had captured the woman's likeness. Pleased with the result, Zadie smiled and motioned for the young woman to come. Dora Grace obeyed and looked at her portrait. At first, she seemed excited and then she burst into tears, grabbed the portrait, and ran into the cabin.

Stunned, Zadie sat for a moment and then followed Dora Grace. "What is wrong? Don't you like it?"

Dora Grace hugged the portrait as though her life depended on it.

Totally confused, Zadie tried to console the woman with a tender touch, but the woman pulled away and wailed. Dora Grace wasn't crying tears. Instead it was a mournful sound that unnerved Zadie to the point that she felt powerless to help. Torn between allowing the woman privacy that she seemed to want and seeking help from the woman's husband, Zadie gave up. I truly don't understand.

She returned to the porch to work on the

picture of the stream with the mountains in the background. But now her heart was not in it. Dora Grace's wails had softened into occasional sobs, but Zadie found that the discomfort of not understanding Dora Grace was unsettling. Zadie forced herself to draw. Why am I here? I'm being asked to share a house that is smaller than my bedroom with two Indians and a man I do not know.

The men came in from the barn smelling like turpentine and varnish. The combination was sickening. "Oh, please wash up with soap and water. I'll fix supper if I know where the food is stored and what I am supposed to prepare. I don't know what you expect me to do or who is supposed to cook the meals."

Duncan shrugged and then looked towards the cabin's interior. "Do I hear Dora Grace?"

Zadie nodded. "I drew her portrait, and I don't know what went wrong. She took it from me and started howling. I tried to talk to her but she pulled away from me. It was as though she wanted to be alone."

"Oh, no. I'll ask Five Paws."

Duncan came back a few minutes later. "This makes no sense, but she thinks you stole her likeness."

"What? That's crazy."

Duncan rolled his palms up. "They are different."

"I noticed."

"I have salted fish and potatoes. Can you make a meal with that?"

Zadie finished packing up her things. "I'll try. Do you have grease I can use for frying?" She stood and grinned at Duncan. "And an egg? I do know how to cook."

***

Duncan spent most of the evening meal trying to explain to Five Paws that Zadie had not taken anything from Dora Grace. Somehow, with the help of a small mirror, they convinced Dora Grace that she was still a whole person.

Duncan waited until everyone had eaten, then he helped Zadie with the dishes.

She handed him the last item to dry and removed her apron. "I'm sorry I caused a problem with Dora Grace. I thought I was doing something nice for her."

"You are very good. That was a fabulous portrait of her." Duncan took Zadie's hand and escorted her to the porch. "But we do need to talk."

"About what?"

"Maybe I made a mistake. I thought you would be happy to have the company of another woman and that she would feel the same. I assumed everything would be fine between you." He held up his hand as though he could hold the air that surrounded them. "Things are different here. Life is different. Having Dora Grace and Five Paws has made my life easier, and I believe it has made their lives better."

Zadie knitted her brow. "I tried to help clean up the kitchen, but Dora Grace pushed me away. At a loss as to what to do, I walked out of the cabin."

"Is that when you hitched the mule?"

Zadie nodded. "I was bored, and I wanted to see where you brought me."

"You can't just do things by yourself around here. There are bears and other animals that roam freely. I don't want you mauled to death."

Zadie heaved a breath. "A bear is more scared of me than I am of him."

"Don't bet on it." He looked at her and raised one hand so his palm faced her. "Wait here for a moment."

When he returned, he was carrying a rifle. "I'll teach you to use this thing, because I already know you aren't going to listen to me when I say to stay home. I can't run around protecting you every time you decide to do something. You need to learn to protect yourself."

Zadie raised her eyebrows. "What makes you think I would purposely be disobedient?"

"You have a very strong independent streak in you. Most women would never dream of wandering around a strange place without an escort."

She took the rifle he passed to her. "I don't want to shoot anything."

"Keep in mind things are different here. Sometimes you only have two choices. Kill or be killed. That's when you will shoot."

He watched as she held the rifle, knowing it would be heavy in her hands. He wasn't certain if it was the weight of the rifle or the gravity of his words, but she seemed somber as she followed him to a pile of wood behind the barn. He rummaged around in a pit that contained his burn pile until he had several old cans. He stacked them on a few pieces of wood. "You're going to practice until you can hit every one, every time. And until you can do that, you have to promise me you will not go anyplace further than where you are in view of the barn, cabin, or house. Do you understand?"

She stuck her tongue out at him.

"Do you promise?"

She stared at him.

He heaved a sigh. "I'm teaching you so you can do what you want with your time. But I'm also teaching you because everyone living out here needs to know how to use a gun."

"I have no intention of ever shooting any

animal or person."

"Fine. I'm glad to know that you won't be aiming this thing at every man, woman, and child in Creed's Crossing or every bird that flies overhead. But if the need arises to use the gun, you must know how use it, and be able to do so without any second thoughts."

He repositioned her hands and then using his feet, he moved hers. "Keep the butt tight to your shoulder. This is not a baby that you are cuddling."

He told her several more things to do and by the time he was finished, he figured she'd never remember to do everything he was saying.

"And that big mean bear will have already eaten me before I get this thing up to my shoulder."

"I'll bring you out here every night until you can do all of it in a split second without thinking. Do you understand how important it is that you not go anywhere without me until you learn to use this?"

She nodded her reply.

"Deep breath, hold, and squeeze."

***

The sound of the rifle in her ear was almost deafening, and she was certain she'd broken her shoulder as the rifle fell from her fingers. She didn't want to cry over the pain because she was furious with Duncan, but tears were trying to well in her eyes.

"Good try." He picked up the rifle, came around behind her, and then positioned the rifle to her shoulder again.

"No. It hurts." She pulled the rifle away.

He removed his shirt. Then he wrapped her shoulder with the cloth. He moved his body tightly to hers.

How dare… But the feel of his chest pressed to her back sent an exciting sensation spiraling through her system. She could barely breathe. He leaned into her and trapped her shoulder between him and the butt of the rifle.

"Now, look down the barrel, and when you're ready, squeeze the trigger."

She took a deep breath, but her heart pounded in her chest, and her hands shook as she tried to aim the riffle. Again, the thing went off with what sounded like an explosion.

"You missed, but you're getting better. We'll try one more time."

She wanted cotton and beeswax plugs in her ears. She wanted him to hold her tight again. Her whole body tingled from his touch.

Five more times he had her shoot the gun. Her ears were ringing from the sound and her shoulder ached. Not once had she managed to hit a can. Never had she failed so miserably at something. I don't want to stay in that little cabin forever because I can't manage to shoot a can. What am I going to do? I must learn to do this!

***

Big fat clouds slipped over the tops of the mountains headed for the ranch. This was one time Duncan didn't want rain. He needed that varnish to dry. He also intended to take Zadie into town.

"How well can you ride a horse?"

"I've ridden all my life. On my fourth birthday, I received a pony. I promise I do know how to ride."

"Good. I'll saddle Rocky up for you and I'll use Five Paws' horse."

Five Paws nodded. "He old and good."

Duncan didn't care as long as he could get to town and back before rain soaked everything. It would be faster to go by horseback than to take the buckboard.

"I'd best change into something suitable for riding." Zadie went to the bedroom and closed the door.

He stepped to her closed door. "Be fast. There are clouds in the sky and we need supplies."

There was no point in waiting for her. He strode to the barn and saddled Rocky. Five Paws' horse didn't have a saddle. The Indian was probably lucky the tribe allowed him to even have a horse. They certainly weren't going to give him a valuable saddle.

Zadie ran out of the house in a skirt that appeared to be split. "I'm ready. Where's the saddle for this horse?"

"He doesn't have one. I'll ride him."

"It doesn't matter. I can ride either horse."

"Bareback?"

She nodded.

"You'll ride Rocky."

The moment he finished with his horse, she slipped her foot into the stirrup and swung into the saddle without any help. It pleased him to see she was comfortable on a horse, especially after last evening's disastrous shooting lessons.

They made excellent time getting into town and he sent her to the butcher for some food for the week. "Choose some bacon and whatever will last us a week, but only what can be kept on a shelf or fixed tonight."

He stepped into the farm supply to pick up a few essential items. Normally he would have enjoyed the social aspect of being in town, but those clouds were moving closer.

Purchasing what he needed, he joined her at the butcher's.

She had bought several things, and it cost more than he had expected. Then they went next door. She did a fast survey of the aisles and chose a few things before concentrating her efforts on canned goods.

Mrs. Barrett looked at him. "When did you find your mail order bride?"

Zadie's head jerked up, and he knew instantly that she was livid by the way she narrowed her eyes and pressed her lips together.

"She's not. She's the daughter of an old family friend who has come to see if she would like to join me here."

"You are keeping her at your ranch and you are not married to her? What will people think?"

Zadie laughed. "They can think whatever they want. Duncan has been an absolute gentleman. As my father says, the apple does not fall far from the tree. His father and my father are as close as brothers. Duncan has allowed me use of the cabin while I'm here."

Mrs. Barrett raised her eyebrows and Zadie raised hers in a defiant return. It was all Duncan could do to keep from laughing at the two women. Mrs. Barrett acted as though she were perfect, but if there was a Commandment that said do not gossip, she would be in big trouble. Or is gossip the same as bearing false witness?

"Are you done?" he asked Zadie.

"Yes. This should be enough."

He paid for everything and they left the store. He packed most of the stuff behind Zadie's saddle and carried some of it. "I'm going to stop at the post office. I'll only be a second. There's no point in you dismounting."

She nodded. "Don't forget to mail my letter."

They stopped at the far end of town. He

ran into the tiny building and came out carrying a few envelopes. "One is for you."

He handed it to her and she pocketed it. He could tell by the name that it wasn't her family.

They picked up speed on the way home. When they arrived at the cabin, he told her to go inside as he unloaded their things onto the porch.

"No. I rode and I can certainly help with the horses."

In the barn, she dismounted and immediately pulled the saddle from Rocky, talking to him the whole time.

"I think Rocky likes you."

"Why wouldn't he? I'm a very likable person."

Duncan laughed as he grabbed the brushes. "And you are better than most women in a saddle."

"I like horses. I wish more people had their personalities. The world would be a better place."

"They are more loyal, and they will let you know if they don't like something." Duncan ran the brush down the hind leg of Five Paws' horse.

"Are you hinting that I'm not being truthful?"

Duncan moved around the horse to groom his far side. "No. But you also haven't said much about being here."

"Back up, baby boy. I can't clean your hooves until you do." Zadie sounded as though she was talking to a toddler.

He watched her check each hoof and then check one again.

"Come look." She held Rocky's back foot in her hand. "I think he's getting ready to throw a shoe."

"Oh, no." He checked the shoe carefully. "I'll drop a fresh nail in it tomorrow. He should be fine, but I'll keep an eye on it."

E. Ayers

If it wasn't one thing, it was another. Ranching was hard work and expensive. He had yet to earn his first dollar, and now he had Zadie to impress. Every month, he received money from his father's business, and he was careful with it, but if she wanted that house filled with furniture, she was going to have to wait. Time was not on his side.

As they left the barn, lightning streaked across the sky, and it began to rain.

***

Zadie raced to the cabin and managed to get there before getting too wet. Duncan had gone back to the barn for something and those few seconds meant the rain drenched him. Standing on the porch, the air smelled of soil and raindrops. It was that wonderful scent of clean air. She gazed at Duncan and took a deep breath. His wet shirt clung to him, showing off his muscled chest and broad shoulders before he peeled the garment off. The slight smattering of blond hair that covered his chest came together and formed a thick stripe that vanished into his pants.

He grinned at her and she could feel the heat rising to her cheeks. He knew she was staring at him, making her wonder if he could read her mind, too. Her cheeks felt as though they were on fire. He held the door for her, and they went inside.

Batter rolls will be easy and quick to make. She opened a jar of tomatoes and poured them into a pan. After adding some dried celery and several slivers from an onion, she stirred the tomatoes and added a few spices. There was a limp carrot on the counter and a small turnip and a tiny beet next to the carrot. She washed all three, pared, and sliced each into super fine strips and added them to the tomatoes. She hoped the strong taste of the tomatoes would cover the taste of other vegetables.

Cooking on his tiny stove took some forethought, as it didn't have a proper oven. But Abilene had warned of the possibility and explained how to manage. Zadie was glad that Abilene had been such a thorough teacher.

She turned to Duncan who was looking out the front door. "Where is your cold cellar?"

"My cold cellar?"

"A cold cellar or springhouse for storing things that need to be kept cold."

He turned and faced her. "I don't have one."

Part of her wondered how he had survived this long, part of her wanted to scream, but instead she smiled. "Any chance you have a large wooden box and a shovel I may use? I can see I have my first real job. I'll make a small cold storage area here and a larger one for the house. This winter we can put ice in it."

He turned away as though he had to watch the rain falling from the sky.

She wasn't certain what to think. She'd seen her father when he had other things on his mind, and to some extent, Duncan acted like a man who was pre-occupied. But when she thought about it more, he acted as though she were a child who had asked for something ridiculous. A little kernel of anger burned inside her. I will never be subservient to a man!

7

Zadie decided the best way to deal with Duncan was to ignore his shortcomings. She remembered Abilene's words. Don't ask for impossible things and expect to actually find them. Many times, Zadie had watched her father leave for long stretches of time. That's when her mother made arrangements to have things handled. And in this case, Zadie knew the way to handle that cold cellar was for her to do it herself.

She went back to cooking the noon meal

and then decided she'd spend the rainy afternoon doing laundry. She certainly had enough dirty clothes after traveling.

As they ate their meal, she asked about a clothesline so that she might hang her things to dry.

Duncan heaved out a deep breath. "I don't have one. I hang stuff over the railing."

Whatever was happening between them wasn't good. "That probably means you don't have clothes pins, either. Do you have a small rope and a few nails that I might use?"

"There's some twine in the barn and a can filled with odd nails. If you tell me exactly what you want, I'll do it."

She forced a smile. "Thank you, but I believe I can string a clothesline. I'm under the impression that you need to spend your time on the house."

"I know you want to be in the house as

soon as possible."

"Creating a clothesline should not be a difficult task. There's no reason why I shouldn't be able to do it." She took a spoonful of her soup. "Is there any chance I'll find a wooden box out there?"

He shook his head. "Nothing of any size."

"I'll see what I can find. With a cold storage area, I'll be able to make better meals. I was hoping to impress you with my culinary skills. Abilene is a wonderful cook and she taught me so much. I even brought a cookbook with me."

He put his spoon down. "I can't fulfill your every little whim. I'm trying to get a ranch going, and it will take time."

"I'm not asking for silver trays. I'm willing to dig my own cold storage area. I know you are busy with the house, and if I had known sooner that you didn't have proper rope for a clothesline, I would have bought it and the pins when we were in town. It's only a few cents. And if you can't afford it, I would have paid for it with the money I have. My father did not send me here as a destitute woman." She dropped her hands to her lap and folded them together, hoping to somehow still her own ire. "I expect you to treat me as an equal. I might not have your strength or your skills, but I don't expect to be coddled like a child."

"Good." He went back to eating.

Duncan's attitude confused her. It also made her more determined to be independent.

After lunch as the rain slowed, Zadie ran to the barn and poked around. She found a bucket of nails, and the twine, but she couldn't find a hammer. She did find a nice wooden box filled with... Picking up one of the metal things inside the box, she looked at it. Threaded. Hmm. Water pipes? There was no clue on the box itself, but the box was a nice size, not too big or too small. It was large enough to hold a wheel of cheese, a few meats, and a jar of milk or cream. And a smaller box meant a smaller hole to dig. Knowing she wouldn't be digging holes in the rain, the box could wait until morning.

She took the roll of twine and several nails back to the house. Standing on a kitchen chair and using a rock as a hammer, she managed to set several nails into the wood around the porch ceiling. Since she didn't have any poles to prevent sagging, she pounded in more nails so that she could string some twine crosswise as support. She carefully knotted and looped the twine around each nail, then pulled on the twine to be certain everything would hold.

Two tubs hung from nails by the back door, and she brought the smaller tub inside. With no washboard or wringer, she had to find the ones she had sent ahead. Back to the barn she went to dig through her crates until she found everything she needed for washing clothes.

She wanted to bring everything she had brought from home into the cabin, but there was practically no room for additional items in that tiny space. Carefully, she selected a few other things that she knew she would need to survive until the house was ready.

In the kitchen, she set the tub on the table and pushed it next to the sink. She'd wash in the tub and rinse in the sink. By the time she began washing, most of the afternoon was gone. She washed her delicate undergarments first, and then started on her clothes. The things she'd worn while traveling were filthy. It took multiple washings and changing the wash water to get them clean. Then she started on Duncan's clothing. All of his shirts were a beige color until she washed them, and the water turned brown. She soaked, washed, wrung, and soaked again. White shirts? She shook her head and knew that would surprise him. I hope he appreciates it.

Dora Grace watched Zadie like a hawk.

Zadie had been trained to teach, and one thing that was drilled into her was to give students information that they could absorb. She pointed to the water. "Water."

Dora smiled.

Zadie said it again slowly. "Wa-a-ter."

Dora Grace repeated the word.

Ecstatic, Zadie pointed into the tub. "Wash in water."

"Wassh."

"Yes!" Zadie smiled.

She had Dora Grace talking, and Zadie didn't want to stop, but she knew to only give tiny bits of information. "Tub." She tapped her nail on the tub. After turning the crank on the wringer, she said, "Wringer." And picked up the soap. "Soap."

Dora Grace parroted the words.

Zadie smiled. She was breaking through the barrier between them.

Zadie took all the wet clothes to the lines on the porch and draped everything the best that she could. It was far from perfect, but at least the clothes were clean.

She mopped the kitchen floor and added a few pieces of wood to the stove. The rain had stopped, but now it was hot and sticky. With the men returning soon looking for supper, Zadie hoped that Duncan's mood had changed.

Once Zadie had everything ready for supper and the washtub put away, she smiled at Dora Grace. The young woman's hair was plastered to her head with perspiration. Zadie retrieved her comb and motioned for Dora Grace to sit in a chair. It took some coaxing, but Zadie finally had the woman where she wanted her. Zadie combed the young Indian woman's hair. At first, it was tangled, but eventually it was like combing through silk. She combed it up and put it in a pretty bun high off the woman's neck. She handed Dora Grace a mirror and the young woman smiled.

Something deep inside told Zadie that Dora Grace loved being dressed like a white woman even though she usually dressed in her tunic with a pair of man's pants under it.

Immediately Dora Grace went back to her piece of material. Whatever Dora Grace was stitching, Zadie could tell the stitches were tiny and even. It wasn't a quilt nor was it a skirt. Zadie shook her head.

That evening, she sat on the porch and opened the letter from Catherine. She was delighted with the portraits of her children that Zadie had left at her parent's home. Even the twins are thrilled with their pictures, which now hang in the nursery. We are going to be moving into our new house next week, and I can't wait. Once we are moved, I will hang their portraits over the parlor mantel. I feel so honored and will always remember that day together.

Zadie quickly realized her days would dissolve into a series of routines. Every morning, she and Dora Grace went to the garden and brought back vegetables to prepare. There were plenty of winter squashes, enough to last through the entire winter if they ate squash every day. But Zadie also found onions and several other things in the garden. She wished someone had asked her before planting everything. Next spring. There's too much of some things and not enough of others.

On Saturday, Zadie and Duncan rode into town for supplies and mail. The man from Laramie came and plastered. The house was beginning to look like a real home. It was a

Sunday evening when she asked Duncan about a stove. "I know you can't afford one at the moment, but I'm willing to buy it. I do have money saved up."

"I will buy the stove. Tell me what you want."

"There's a wonderful stove made by Excelsior, but it's expensive, and I have no idea how much more would have to be paid in shipping."

"Just tell me what it costs."

"About twenty-seven dollars. The Barretts have a picture of it in their store."

"That's horrendously expensive."

"I know. I thought that, too. There are others for twenty-two dollars, but they are not as nice."

He dropped his forehead into his hand. "I'm sorry, Zadie. I'm feeling the pressure of trying to provide and not giving you credit for the things that you have done."

"I know you've been trying to finish the house before winter sets in, and I know you want us to live as a couple. But you don't always allow me into your life, and you seem to get upset when I do things on my own."

"There are some things that you are doing that are considered a man's job. Yet, you insist on doing them."

"If I can do them, then why not?"

"Because it means I'm not doing them for you. I'm trying to finish the house."

"I realize that. And I realize that I am asking for things that you have done without."

"Ranching takes up my time and the house is adding more. I want to be a good husband and provider. My father ran his herring business and my mother took care of the house. Maybe I never paid close enough attention." He rolled his palms up. "I'm trying to do the most important things first."

"My father never did anything in the house. It was my mother's job to tell him, then he would arrange to have it done."

"It's not like that here. There's no one to ask. It all falls on me."

"I do understand." She reached over and touched his arm. "Duncan, I don't care what is labeled for a man or a woman. What matters is that the job is completed." She smiled at him. "I'm willing to help with the house or anything that needs to be done."

"But if you do it, then I feel guilty for not doing it."

She folded her arms over her chest. "Please don't be that way. If I can't do something, I will tell you."

"You are a fantastic artist, and I'm keeping you here in the middle of Wyoming, away from your art, your family, and making you do things that you don't want to do. I'm also failing to prove to you that I can be a good husband."

Zadie almost choked on her coffee as she giggled. "When I see you without your shirt, I know you will make a wonderful husband."

"Then maybe I should go shirtless more often."

"You are rather vain." She giggled.

"If I didn't wear a shirt, you'd have less laundry." He grinned and took her hand. "Let's go for a walk."

"No shooting lessons tonight?"

"You are horrible with a gun. I'm not sure you'll ever be able to hit the side of a barn."

"A barn is much bigger than a little can, and I can't imagine a vicious chipmunk attacking me." She gave his hand a squeeze as they stepped off the porch. "You really aren't being fair to me, because you've never allowed me to point the gun at the barn. I'm willing to bet I could hit it if I tried very hard."

"Don't even think about it. You are not going to put holes in my barn's roof."

***

A few days later, cold air blew across the land, and Duncan was pleased he and Five Paws had brought the cattle down near the house when they had. Together, they had managed to build two of the four chimneys before the cold air had settled over the land. A thick gray blanket of clouds rolled above the ranch and Duncan expected snow, but none came.

It was clear the day he took Zadie into town. The ride was lovely as the trees still were holding their autumn colors. He needed to order the stove, and she was eager to have it. They would be able to move into the house soon and leave the Indians to enjoy the cabin by themselves.

Zadie had never really asked for anything other than that stove, and Duncan was determined to buy it for her. He was also giving up on the idea of keeping her at home until she learned to use the rifle. He hated to admit it, but he was coming to the conclusion that the most she'd ever do was fill the air with bullets, and that would alert him.

The cabin was so much cleaner now, and even the windows sparkled, as they never had. It had been a long time since he'd seen shirts that were white, blue, and the one that was green. In fact, he'd forgotten it was green. Her cooking was delicious, but even her cookies and other treats couldn't compare to those gooey sticky buns from the bakery in town. He made a mental note to buy some. But did he dare try to tell her that he loved those sticky buns? Would she learn to bake them if I told her? She's never going to want to marry me if I can't figure out how to treat her better. It's not enough to just build a house for her... I don't want her to leave.

Zadie's voice broke the quiet of the sounds of nature and horses' hooves on the dirt road. "Is anything wrong?"

"Thinking about all the things that still need to be done to the house, and..." He stared off into the distance. "I want you to be happy here."

A week later, after Duncan and Zadie had been to town again, they finished their evening meal and took their coffee to the main room of the cabin. He placed his cup on the tiny table between the two chairs. "Five Paws and I are almost done with the house. As soon as the cooking and heating stoves arrive, along with the shipment of coal from Montana, we can move into the house."

"But there's no furniture." Zadie sat in the primitive rocking chair that creaked with each forward movement.

He shrugged. "I can take the bed and our table and chairs. Real furniture will have to wait until I can sell some of my cattle at market this spring."

"Then I shall persevere."

"That's it? No excitement, no joy?"

"I've survived a lot of the challenges of living here. I'm certain I can manage a few more months without furniture. It's an empty building that needs lamps, not lanterns. It will take awhile to turn it from a house into a home." She gave him what he'd grown to recognize as a forced smile. "I'll look forward to doing that."

"I'm glad you are here. Do you feel better about coming here?"

"Yes. I truly enjoy our evening walks, but

life on a ranch is different. I'm learning to adapt."

"We can walk when we're finished our coffee. It's a beautiful evening and not too cold."

"Before we wander off, I have a letter from my mother burning a hole in my pocket"

He grinned. "I used to do the same thing with your letters. I would save them until this time of night to read them. I wanted to savor every word."

"From me?"

"Yes, from you. You'd make me laugh."

"I'm still waiting for all the social events."

He chuckled as he lifted his cup. "When we get our furniture, we'll plan a party."

"Is that when I'll meet our neighbors?" She pulled a letter from her pocket, started to read, and gasped. The letter dropped from her fingers and she turned whiter than a new shirt.

"What is wrong?"

Zadie burst into tears.

Duncan didn't know how to console her, so he sat patiently to see what she might do or say.

Finally she looked at him and mumbled. "My father has died. I must go home."

He went to her and wrapped his arms around her. She sobbed uncontrollably on his shoulder as he held her tight. "Yes. I understand. I'll go to town tomorrow and see about your tickets."

She cried until his shirt was soaked. He knew she was close to her family. He'd never experienced that kind of pain, but he knew he'd be upset if he received word that his father had died. Men hid their tears. They would chop wood or do something to keep from crying, but women let their tears flow unchecked. "As the only child, you must go to your mother."

"I have my own money to return home," she squeaked out between sobs.

"No, my darling. I'll pay for your tickets home. You need to be with your mother and Abilene." He knelt before her. "I wish I could go with you, but I cannot leave the ranch."

***

Zadie spent the rest of the evening in a muted fog as she packed a trunk for home. Her father had not been well when she left for Wyoming, and now she hated herself for not staying behind. It was her fault her father had died. If she had been there, she could have somehow prevented it. Guilt dug its way clear to her soul.

Her trip home only took a few days. But by the time she had arrived, she was exhausted. Ole Bill met her at the train station with her father's carriage. And when they reached the house, a black swag hung around the door. She had missed her father's funeral, but she was still needed.

Ole Bill brought her trunk into the house and carried it up the stairs to what had once been her room. She thanked him and dropped a few coins into his hand. Her mother was in her room wearing widow weeds. Her skin color was ashen and her eyes were red from crying. Abilene wasn't much better.

Aside from Zadie's initial shock, she'd not taken time to grieve. Now was not the time to fall apart. She washed up and then went to the kitchen where she managed to fix some food. It was obvious that Abilene was just as grief stricken, for the kitchen was in disarray.

Zadie pulled herself together and worked hard.

Two days later, Zadie took her mother to the law office to listen to the reading of the Will. There wasn't much money. If her mother didn't sell the house, she would quickly run out of the little bit of cash that was left. That night Zadie wrote to Duncan.

***

Duncan finished the house and wondered if Zadie would ever return. He knew he had failed. He just wasn't certain how. Maybe he hadn't given her enough freedom. I failed to appreciate the things that she did. Failed to thank her each time.

She had left thirty dollars with a note in the bedroom. It was supposed to be payment for the stove. He had paid for it when he'd ordered it, but he hadn't told her. Should I send the money to her or keep it? He hadn't decided. It was almost as much money as his father sent each month. Finally, he made the decision to keep it, for he was certain that he'd find a letter waiting for him, asking that he ship her crates back.

He walked to the barn and checked Rocky's hoof. The shoe was loose again, and Duncan didn't want to continue to sink nails into it. It was as though the shoe no longer fit the horse. The farrier would be coming in another week. But Rocky wasn't the kind of horse to stay cooped up. He'd already kicked the sides of his stall a dozen times, he'd bray and throw a tantrum as though he were a child who was being punished.

"Come on, Rocky. This crisp, cold day is perfect for a ride."

Duncan saddled Rocky, certain the horse

understood every word, for he behaved himself. Once outside, Rocky wanted to gallop, but Duncan wasn't going to allow that with a bad shoe. They headed towards the mountains, and Duncan realized how some men could become drifters. The way he felt, he didn't want to return to his ranch. His heart was breaking into pieces and falling into his gut. You have to come back, Zadie. I will do everything in my power to make everything perfect for you.

Zadie was everything he wanted and more than he realized he desired. Her beautiful dark hair tumbled past her derrière. She may not have been as curvy as some women, but what she had was certainly appealing to him. She never complained about her chores and often did things that he wished that she hadn't. He thought about the little box that she had buried in the dirt to hold a few dairy products and a small amount of meat. She created a haphazard covering for it made of firewood and tied a rope to the box so she could lift it. He dug her a big cold cellar not far from the kitchen door of the house with steps so she could walk into it. It was like a small underground room. One wall was solid rock and the other walls were lined in boards, as was the ceiling.

But ice was a problem. There was no iceman to bring it. He had to make his own blocks. At least, he knew it would be made with clean water from the well. But he had no idea how much he would need to last through a whole summer.

He wrote his mom and asked if there was anything he had missed when he built the house. She told him a clothesline in the backyard and sent him a picture from a catalog for a drying rack that hung from the ceiling and could be raised and lowered. She said it was perfect for inclement weather and for a woman's delicates.

He needed two small pulleys for that clothesline. He could buy those at the farm supply. The rest of the drying rack was made with wood, rope, and a few eyebolts. Mentally he ticked off the things he needed to buy in town and calculated the cost. He waxed and waned over Zadie's returning. He wanted to believe that she would, but he feared that she would not. But if she returned, he wanted everything perfect for her. If she didn't... He didn't want to think about that.

Movement caught his eye and he reined Rocky to a halt.

There, at the far end of the field before the land dipped into a ravine, was a lone, white-tailed deer. Duncan grabbed for his rifle. "Easy, Rocky. This will be meat for weeks."

The deer looked up, as if to smell the air,

and then went back to eating. Duncan wanted a clean shot. He didn't want to maim and then have to chase the wounded thing for miles, especially with Rocky's shoe. Duncan edged the horse closer, and when the deer looked up again, it showed signs of bolting. Taking aim, he fired, and watched. The animal ran for a few feet and stumbled. The deer breathed its last breath as Duncan rode to it.

Thrilled with his kill, he laid the carcass over Rocky's rump and headed back to the cabin. It took a few minutes to hang the deer. Then he took care of Rocky and carefully checked his hoof. Relieved that there was no change to the horse's shoe or hoof, he headed for the cabin.

He wanted to tell Zadie of his good fortune, but she wasn't there. He missed her scent, the smell of soap that filled the cabin after she had bathed, her quirky sense of humor, and her fierce independence. But mostly he missed the quiet evenings, watching her draw. He missed her and wanted to share his life with her. Now she was gone and might never come back. His only hope was that so far she had not written to tell him to ship her crates home.

He walked into his bedroom and picked up the barrette she had left behind and rolled it around in his palm. Come back, Zadie. I love you.

Friday night, Duncan opened a letter from Zadie. He'd postponed it for as long as he could, carried the letter around in his pocket, letting it burn a hole into his heart. Instead of being certain that he'd savor her every word, he was positive this would be her final goodbye. Dreading what she might say and having already decided he had no way to change her mind, he'd be forced to accept her staying in Franklin.

He slipped his penknife under the fold

and slit the envelope. His heart pounded as he opened the letter inside.

My dear Duncan,

I have arrived home to a total mess. Momma hasn't done anything except cry, and Abilene isn't much better. The only good thing about my return is that my wool skirts are ready.

Poppa didn't leave much for my mother. He only had a small insurance policy and his bank account wasn't much better. Once I am finished paying all of his bills, there won't be much in the bank. I'm afraid my mother will have to sell the house to survive. It is a lovely home, and it is much too big for her and Abilene. She knows she must move and is now lamenting over leaving her home in addition to adjusting to Poppa's passing.

I was surprised to see that my

father entrusted Abilene to me, along with a small sum of money to take care of her. In truth, my father left me in charge of everything, including my mother's money. At first, I was stunned. But watching Momma in her present state, I can see why he did it, for she has fallen completely apart.

My father's sister, Aunt Helen, lives in Windsor, Virginia, and she brought bits of sunshine into the reading of The Will. Poppa's solicitor was quite upset and didn't find it funny when my father bequeathed his sister his precious moon clasps. My Aunt Helen burst into laughter and I couldn't hold back my giggles. Momma cried and said that was so like him to leave them to his sister.

We were supposed to produce these moon clasps at the solicitor's office, and being there is no such thing, we couldn't. Many a family gathering had me trying to find them. I must have been around ten when I figured out it was the way the adults removed the children from a conversation. These "clasps" are family heirlooms that have gone through several generations. Apparently I caught on quicker than my aunt did, for my grandfather often had her hunting for these things well into her teens.

Anyway, we all had to sign a paper that said it was merely a family joke, and no such clasps existed. I still think the solicitor thinks we are lying. No one can grab the moon and hold it in place.

After the reading, we were standing outside and Aunt Helen's daughter, Lucy, who is only a few years younger than I am, laughed and said, "Those precious moon clasps are encrusted with diamonds and blue sapphires in solid gold. Why was your father so careless that he'd managed to misplace them all the time?"

That sent us into another round of merriment, for she, too, had gone looking for those clasps while visiting.

Duncan mumbled, "I know where you got your sense of humor, Zadie."

I've not even had a chance to mourn except at night when I am alone in my room. That's when the tears flow unchecked. I do not know if they flow because I've lost my father or because I am no longer in Wyoming with you. It seems I quickly became accustomed to life with you.

My friend Catherine has moved into her new home. She has offered to buy some of Momma's furniture, but I am thinking that you can use many pieces for your house. Catherine's husband will be buying my father's carriage and his two horses.

My father also owned his office building in town and that must be sold. Our mayor is trying to entice another doctor to come to Franklin. If the mayor succeeds, I won't have to worry about accounting for every instrument and drug that my father owned, or all of his patients' records. The new doctor could buy the office with monthly payments which would make it easier on him, and that would greatly help Momma by giving her a small monthly income.

I don't know how long it will take to handle everything here. My mother needs me and there is so much to do.

E. Ayers

Right now I'm trying to take care of the house, do the shopping, fix the meals, clear my father's personal possessions, and sort through all his papers. And I'm doing it with a heavy heart.

Please do not forget me.

Zadie

"How could I ever forget you, Zadie? You left a burr in my blanket that won't go away."

8

Five Paws came into the main room. "Were you talking to me?"

"I think since Zadie left, I've started talking to myself."

"You love her, but you never tell her. Women want to know they be loved."

Duncan nodded. "She always kept me at arm's length. Never let me get any closer to her."

"You try? You tell her you want kiss and more?"

Duncan's heart sank. "No."

"You need to tell her such things. Make her want you. It took many moons make Dora Grace want. She young and afraid. I wait, but she good. Yes?"

Duncan smiled. "Yes, she is good. She loves you."

"We miss our family, but this good. She love cabin and stove."

"She's learned much from Zadie. Her cooking has improved."

"White man's food different. She happy see deer."

"She wasn't the only one." That feeling of pride swelled inside of him. "That will give us meat for quite a while."

The next day Duncan walked through his house and looked at everything. The walls were finished, and so was all the wood trim. He ran his hand over the smooth plaster wall. It was a soft white with the slightest tinge of pink to the finish. She'll like this.

At least he had managed two of the chimneys before the cold forced him to stop. He had installed Zadie's expensive woodstove in the kitchen. Above the kitchen, he had placed a small heater that would warm the bathing room and also give hot water. But in the parlor, he fitted the fireplace with an ornate coal burner. It was cast iron and decorated in tiles, and it had cost almost as much as her stove.

He figured the coal might be a better choice, as he didn't want to remove every tree from his property trying to heat a house. Satisfied that he couldn't do much more, he closed the door behind him and went to check on his cattle.

His bulls were in one pasture along with his breeding cows. The steers were in another. With luck he'd have enough steers to begin selling and making a profit. But a few conversations with other ranchers made him realize he'd need to buy some chickens and maybe a few ducks. Being self-sufficient was important, and so far, that hadn't happened. I can't do it all at once.

He pulled the collar up on his coat as cold air blasted his neck. He knew to let his hair and his beard grow in the Wyoming winter. The worst of the cold was ahead of him.

He reached for a few split logs and chopped them into sizes suitable for the cabin's stove. When he was done, he had two large armloads of wood. The smaller pieces were usually used in the morning to get the hot embers going so a log or two could be added. Dora Grace would get upset if the stove was too hot for whatever she wanted to make, yet that stove also heated the house. It was a balancing act between cooking and heating. The little cabin was tight and kept the cold out. He dropped the wood into the barrel he kept in the kitchen and went to his bedroom.

He picked up Zadie's barrette and held it in his hand. That was all she had left behind except for her boxed things in the barn. They were hers and he had never opened them. The little barrette was something he'd found on the floor by the bed. She must have dropped it as she packed her things. He sat on his bed and reread her letter. Come back, Zadie, I miss you. I need you, too.

***

Zadie wasn't thinking when she left Creed's Crossing. She had brought her clothes with her, but none were suitable for a family in mourning. Ethel had instantly made

Zadie's mom two black dresses and one for Abilene, but considering Zadie's hatred of black, the seamstress had made Zadie a very dark navy blue dress trimmed in black and a charcoal dress trimmed in a pale lavender. Then she made Zadie a cape of navy blue wool that was trimmed in charcoal and had been piped with the purple hue in her charcoal dress. Zadie needed to thank the woman and settle the debts the family had accrued.

The first chance Zadie had, she went into town. So many people stopped to give their condolences and tell her how wonderful her father's funeral had been. They were sorry that she had missed it. To some extent, she was glad she had missed it, and in a way, she was remorseful that it was over a week after he had died before she even knew about his death. Part of her felt as though she should have been home. Now she was picking up the pieces of her mother's life, and she had no idea what she was going to do with them.

She opened the door to Ethel's shop and stepped inside. The familiar scent of sewing machine oil and cloth greeted her. "Hello!"

Ethel came out from a back room. "Zadie, how are you? And how is your mother?"

"I'm afraid my mother is engrossed in her mourning. She does nothing but cry, and she refuses to receive guests. I have assumed that she needs this time alone, for she is adrift at sea without my poppa."

"Oh, how sad. But you look as though you are doing well."

"Maybe. I have not had time to grieve. There is so much that needs to be done."

"You have plenty of time. But what about your young man, I thought you were going to marry him?"

"I'm hoping. Of course I wasn't expecting

to lose my father. Now my mother needs me. It's all so confusing."

Ethel nodded. "It was so sad. I heard the commotion and stepped out of the shop. Apparently your father was crossing the street to meet with Rex Everett." She wiped a tear from her cheek. "Dr. Larkford clutched his chest and fell to the ground. It was so sudden. We're all struggling to deal with the loss. I'm sure you know that everyone loved him."

"I believe Poppa was trying to hide a heart condition from us. He blamed his problems on his age." She removed her gloves and swiped at the tears that were trying to spill down her cheeks. "I should have never left."

"Now, don't go blaming yourself over your father's heart. Have a seat. I was fixing a pot of tea when you came. There's enough for both of us."

Zadie sat and chatted with Ethel for most of the afternoon. It was good to talk to another woman. Ethel was widowed when her children were babies, and she had opened the shop to survive. Almost thirty years later, she still had her shop and plenty of work.

"I need to settle all debts so that I can clear my father's accounts."

Ethel retrieved her box where she kept all her client's records. On a five by eight card was the name Gregory Larkford and under it was probably twenty some years of purchases. "Eighteen dollars and thirty-four cents. I didn't charge for Abilene's. I used some remnants, and hers was so plain it was easy to make.

Zadie pulled a pouch from her pocket and handed Ethel twenty dollars. "Keep the change."

She stood and looked around. She needed more warm clothing for Wyoming, for she had been warned of the bitterly cold winters there. She also knew she would not go back there wearing mourning clothing. A pretty blue wool caught her eye, as did a heavy dark blue twill. "My split skirts are perfect for riding. I think I need several. And this denim twill is wonderful. Keeping house is a messy job."

Ethel laughed. "You have been spoiled by Abilene. I think everyone in town envies the fact that you still have a slave."

"Abilene is not a slave!"

"Zadie, have a seat. Seems there are some facts you don't know." Ethel poured another cup of tea and put her closed sign on the door. "Abilene was a slave. She belonged to your granddaddy. But she refused to leave when the war was over."

Zadie swallowed. All she had ever heard was that Abilene was her father's nanny.

"How do you know this?"

"Because your daddy and I are from the same area, Courtland."

Zadie listened to Ethel with a feeling of disbelief.

"When the war ended, Abilene never left. She didn't just love your father - she loved your grandfather as well. Her son is only a year older than your daddy, and rumor had it that he's your father's half-brother."

Zadie swallowed her tea and put the cup down. Her hands were shaking. Abilene was my grandfather's mistress?

Ethel went on to tell Zadie details about the War that she had never learned - stories about the people in Franklin, carpetbaggers, a slave by the name of Nat Turner who lived just a sort distance away, and even Ole Bill.

"I never heard my father tell of anyone around here who was cruel to his slaves. Nat

Turner scared many an owner into being nice to their Negroes."

Ethel shook her head. "But it wasn't like that for most of them. You ask Ole Bill to show you his scars from where he was whipped. He was young and defiant. But Abilene was just a girl and a house slave when the War broke out. She had her son and your father was a babe." She sipped at her tea.

"Your granddaddy took good care of Abilene's son and sent him to Hampton Normal and Agricultural Institute so that he got an education. That boy even returned for your daddy's funeral. Although I don't think there was any love between the two boys, I'd place my bets that there was some jealousy. But I'm certain Simon came back to show his respect, not for your daddy, but for his mother." Ethel stopped for a moment and stared into nothingness before taking another sip of her tea. "Those two men looked like peas in pod except instead of your father's straight hair, Simon's is curled, but not kinky. It's soft like his momma's. Simon's skin is almost as white as yours."

Zadie was stunned. The color of Abilene's skin said she was mixed. It wasn't something that Zadie could ever ask about, and she realized that Abilene might not know for certain. Times had changed and things were different now. But the more Zadie pondered the situation the more introspective she became. Most Negroes were still considered worthless humans. Yet her father swore that the only difference was the color of their skin.

That made her think of Dora Grace and Five Paws. They were good people. But they weren't at all like the Negroes. The Indians were different. Uncivilized in so many ways. It wasn't as though she had never seen a man's bare chest, but Five Paws walked around virtually naked, as though it were perfectly acceptable.

At least Duncan keeps his chest covered. Well, not always. The thought of his naked chest stirred something in her. He did things to her - created feelings in her that she'd never felt before.

She finished her cup of tea and went to the shelves where Ethel stacked her bolts of fabric, hoping for a much-needed moment to compose herself. There were too many thoughts flitting through her mind, and most of them were tinged with sadness. She fingered a heavy wool.

"You are not planning on wearing black when you return to Wyoming?" Ethel's question pulled Zadie from her thoughts.

"No. I'm on a ranch in the middle of nowhere. Cows do not care if I'm in mourning."

Another bolt of blue material had seized Zadie's attention. "This. Could you make me a split skirt and a jacket to match? And I will need a blouse."

Ethel showed Zadie a pattern. "I can do this in white wool or something lightweight." Ethel pulled another bolt of fabric. "Flannel. This is lovely for nightgowns or shirts."

Zadie picked out several more items and then left the shop. Her funds were no longer unlimited, but she was already forming a plan for her mother and Abilene. Talking them into it might take some work.

***

Snowflakes swirled and fell to the ground. The grass hid under the layer of snow, but cattle were too stupid to dig for it. Duncan had to feed them.

E. Ayers

He quickly used a few nails and some scrap wood to make two troughs to hold the grain, and then dragged them to the two pastures. Using buckets, he filled both troughs with corn, and immediately the cattle happily began eating. Then he took the buckboard to a hayrick, and with the pitchfork, he loaded the buckboard. There were more heads to feed this year, and last year's snow wasn't as deep. He'd hoped for a better harvest, but the summer had started out dry. There was wheat, although the corn wasn't as plentiful.

He thought back to the corn he had eaten this past summer. It had been delicious. And when his field corn had been past its prime, the corn that had been planted in the garden had begun to produce. A few weeks later, all of the corn was drying on the stalks. Now his cattle were enjoying themselves.

He'd been lucky to buy a thrasher last

summer from a man who had attempted to homestead but had given up. It wasn't like the expensive ones, but it was enough for him to bag wheat for storage. He'd hoped to sell some wheat, but now he was feeding it to his livestock.

Thick gray clouds hid the sun, but he knew it was dinnertime for him. He realized his mistake as he tossed his pitchfork into the buckboard. The cattle should have been fenced where his hayricks stood. Next year. He pushed the disparaging thoughts to the side as he made his way to the cabin where Dora Grace would be fixing a meal. The scent of roasting deer meat filled the air. Zadie had taught Dora Grace how to make gravy, but as many times as the young woman tried, it was lumpy. This was one day he didn't care. Breakfast had been cornbread and after working hard all morning in the cold, he was more than ready to eat a hearty meal. He was trying to do all the right things, but his heart was broken without Zadie.

***

Dora Grace was wearing her traditional clothes, which kept her warm, but she often pulled her hair into a bun much like the one that Zadie wore. Today she wore braids. Her tummy bulged and she frequently talked about the baby that would be coming this winter. Proper women never said a word about such things, but Indians didn't seem to have any inhibitions.

After a filling midday meal of deer roast and potatoes, Duncan sat with his pen and paper and began to compose his letter to Zadie.

My dearest Zadie,

To say I've missed you is an understatement. You stay on my mind. So many times, I have turned, ready to tell you some small thing, and expected you to still be here. Instead, you are far away.

The house is finished, but since it is only the three of us, I'm staying in the cabin. It is fine for now, although I miss my privacy. I wish I were not hearing the sounds of matrimony, for that makes me long for the day when you willingly become my wife.

Either you have not written, or I've not received your letters. I only read the first one you wrote when you arrived home. I worry about you and how you are doing.

There's not much happening here, for it has snowed. It was deep enough to bury most of the grass in the field. I've taken the livestock corn and wheat from my harvest. It's been bitter cold, and it's

E. Ayers

early in the season. I sleep in my union suit and my socks.

We all went to bed early the other night and when I awakened, the stove had gone cold. The pump froze, as did the coffee that was left in the pot. Yes, it gets cold here. I keep thinking about those dozen children you want. That would be a nice way of staying warm.

I ordered coal for the house. It is supposed to come today but with the snow, it might be delayed.

I've also made blocks of ice for the cold cellar. The first one I made was too big and too heavy. I had to make smaller blocks. They are still heavy but these will work better. I lined the floor with hay.

Dora Grace often uses the grain I grew. She pounds the wheat berries, and she uses them in baking. It makes things look brown and I can't say it's added to the taste. I had to stop her from putting it in the oatmeal. She says they are all grains and it should not matter. You need to teach her more.

Life is quiet this time of year. Come back. I miss you.

He signed it simply with his name, read through it once, and decided it was a little foolish, but he didn't care.

He put it in an envelope and left it near the door on a small shelf that contained a lantern. He'd take it to town the next time he went.

***

Zadie had more to do than she could handle. Sitting at her father's desk, she began to make a checklist with notes of the things she still had to do. She had closed most of her father's accounts, but had not found a bill for coal deliveries. She would have to inquire in town. Too many times her father was paid for his service with another service. It was confusing. The passion inside of her had burned out. She was numb and decided she would tackle the rest of it in the light of day.

After walking through the house, she made her way upstairs. But as she approached her bedroom, she heard her mother's soft cries. She knocked on her mother's door. "Momma." She turned the cut-glass handle and opened the door. Her mother was sitting at her vanity. "You need to stop crying. Poppa wouldn't want to see you this upset. It would break his heart."

Her momma dabbed her eyes with a pretty hankie.

Zadie wrapped her arms around her mother. "You need to sleep. It will help."

"It doesn't. When I'm alone, it's twice as lonely. What am I going to do?"

"Momma, let's face one problem at a time. I'm settling Poppa's accounts. Then we'll worry about how much is left for you. But you will need to sell this house. It is too big for you and Abilene, and I've already told you that it will cost too much to heat it. Besides, who do you think will haul all the coal around for you? Abilene might be able to do it this year, but what about next? She's getting older. Someday we will be her nursemaids. Will you be able to handle that?"

Her mother shook her head.

"And you won't be able to afford the amount of coal needed to keep this place warm. Momma, you have to listen to reason. You can't stay here forever."

Her mother dissolved into another round of tears. "How will I face my friends?"

"They will understand. You are luckier than most women who are widowed." Zadie sighed. "I'm trying, Momma. I'll find you a nice house that is smaller." And where will I find such a house? It makes more sense if you would go west with me. I can't keep running back here over every little problem. She kissed her mother goodnight and went to her room.

Zadie sat by her front window and looked over the town. The moon failed to cast enough light to even see the river, and very few houses had their lights lit. She opened her window just enough to listen to any sounds, but all she heard were some cats fighting. Aside from the caterwauling, there was only cool evening air coming into her bedroom.

The ranch flitted through her mind. The house Duncan was building would be perfect for a family. It was slightly larger than what Catherine and her husband had bought, but

Duncan's house was well laid out and seemed more spacious with plenty of bedrooms.

Alone in her own room, usually Zadie allowed herself to cry, but tonight, the tears were not coming. She undressed, slipped into her nightgown, and sat by her front window watching the fog roll into town. Finding a house here in Franklin for Momma is impossible. There is no other option.

She wanted to talk to Duncan and tell him all that had happened. But when she thought about writing, her mind went blank. Maybe tomorrow night.

***

Duncan rode into town, hoping for a letter from Zadie, but there was nothing. He went to the bakery, but his favorite buns were still baking. He crossed the street to the farm supply.

E. Ayers

"Howdy," he called as he stepped inside.

"Where's your Indian?" a man answered.

"I left him at home with his wife. He's got plenty to keep him busy." Duncan picked up a can of saddle soap. "I need this."

"What happened to your woman? Did you scare her away?" Ted Barrett laughed.

The old man in the corner exploded in laughter, as though it was the funniest thing he'd heard in ages.

"I sure hope not. Things were going well until she got a letter from home. Her father died and she was needed there. Can't fault her for returning home."

Ted shook his head. "That's a durn shame. She was a pretty lass. Those big brown eyes of hers were enough to make any man look twice."

"As long as no one does anything more than admire…" Duncan raised his eyebrows at Ted.

"Don't go looking at me. I'm a happily married man. But a man's going to notice a pretty woman."

"She's not just pretty - she's smart, and she's an amazing artist. She can look at something and then draw it like that." Duncan snapped his fingers. "I've only gotten one letter from her since she went home. She talked about returning to Creed's Crossing and about the mess that she was handling. Her father left her in charge of his estate."

"That's a man's job."

Duncan held out his palm. "She's the only child."

"Then you don't know if she's coming back."

Duncan shook his head and took a seat on a barrel near the counter. "I've been worried since the day she left. She came and the house wasn't finished. I've got my Indians living with me and to be honest, they are wonderful people. But miss --"

"Indians?" a man asked.

"Yes. Without Five Paws, I don't think I would have made it through this past season. Even now he helps. And Dora Grace keeps me fed better than I could manage on my own."

The old man spoke up, "You got dem dogs living with you?"

Duncan could feel his hackles rising. "Yes, sir. Without them I'd be packing my bags for home. Five Paws has become my right hand. I couldn't ask for better help or a nicer person."

The old man shook his head. "Still say they are dogs. Ain't gonna find one of them hanging around my place. I'll shoot 'em."

Duncan blew out a breath. There were plenty more people who felt the same way about the Indians. At least, Zadie accepted them. He knew in the beginning that she was scared of them. He wasn't exactly friendly towards them until he got to know them. All he'd ever heard were stories about the terrible things that they did. And that was all Zadie had known until she met them. He thought about how she and Dora Grace were starting to become friends and how much Zadie had taught the young woman.

He paid for the saddle soap and went to the dry goods store. When he found Bill Barrett's wife, he asked, "Do you have things for new babies? We're going to have one at my place."

Mrs. Barrett raised her eyebrows. "Is that why we haven't seen your young lady?"

Duncan stifled his anger. "No. Her father died. She had to return home long enough to handle his estate. It's for my foreman's wife."

It cost him two dollars, but he bought several baby items. He went to the bakery, bought his favorite sticky buns, and stopped by the butcher for some bacon. As he stepped out of the butcher's, he noticed that mail was being delivered from Laramie. He returned to the post office. There was a letter from Zadie, and he couldn't wait to read it.

A short distance from town, he reined Rocky to a halt and dismounted. Sitting on an outcropping of rock, he pulled Zadie's letter from his pocket and began to read.

My dearest Duncan,

Living in Franklin has been difficult, except for being able to purchase more clothing that I will need in Creed's Crossing, and seeing my friend Catherine and her new home. I have sent several crates of furniture to you. They would not give me a delivery date because of snow. I hope you will like everything.

Please tell me how Rocky is doing. I have worried about his shoe.

Duncan snickered. He had kept a close eye on that shoe until the farrier came, but he never once worried about it. Zadie had fussed over Rocky and had constantly checked that hoof. "Rocky, you had her hoodwinked. And you knew it."

Rocky lifted his head as if to nod.

"Next thing you know, she'll be tying ribbons in your mane. You better be careful or she'll have you looking like a mare." He went back to reading.

I still must wait on the sale of our family home here. There is great promise that my father's office will be sold as well, but that transaction can be handled by others. Although, I would feel better if it sells before I leave. My father's house is quite large. I have considered selling it at a reduced price, but my mother needs the money she'll receive from the sale. I have placed advertisements for the house in newspapers as far away as Suffolk, Norfolk, Emporia, and Richmond, Virginia, as well as Elizabeth City, North Carolina. Surely someone will respond, for it is a lovely home.

The leaves on the trees are starting to turn colors. I've been gathering leaves and pressing them. So many things I took for granted do not exist there. I noticed the difference on my return trip. The further east I came, the more trees I saw. As I walked to the cemetery the other day, I realized I was wishing I could push all the trees away as though there were too many. And instead of looking off to the mountains, I only see as far as the next stand of trees.

Most nights, I leave my window slightly open at night to allow for any breeze. The temperature rarely dips very low and my blankets keep me warm. I listen to the sounds of the town that never seems to sleep for more than a few minutes. I never knew how quiet it could be until I was on your ranch. Now Franklin seems noisy. I hear a tugboat's bell or the train's whistle, a dog barking, a toddler's cry, or a carriage going through town. Yes, it is different in Wyoming.

Duncan decided she sounded homesick for the ranch, yet she had not actually said when she was returning to him. Why is she giving me furniture? Why didn't she sell it if her mother needed the money? Wouldn't her mother need it in another house? No, she's coming back to me. Her letter had left him with more questions and still hadn't answered the most important question that he had. Are you coming back to marry me, Zadie?

Part Three

9

Abilene sat on her trunk with her arms crossed over her chest and her lips pressed into a thin line.

"Zadie, you talk to her," Zadie's mom implored.

Zadie sat next to Abilene on the trunk. "This is your last chance to change your mind. I told you I'd give you the money that Poppa left for you if you want to stay in Virginia with your son."

"I already made up my mind. I'm not leaving you or your momma. You'll be spitting out babies soon enough, and I'm going be there to rock them. Besides, your momma don't know anything about having babies. She had chloroform." Abilene made a face. "I'm not going to leave you in that wild place to have your babies with no one around. You just wait and see. You'll be glad I'm there with you."

"But I don't want to take you from your son."

"Are you trying to tell me that you don't want me?"

"Oh no, Abilene, but you're going to be too far from your son to see him when we go to Wyoming."

"Well, you came home when you had to be here."

"True." Zadie nodded.

"I'm going with you. I don't want any more discussion. I've made my decision."

Zadie walked through the house one more time, but there was nothing left. Every footfall echoed in the empty rooms. The movers had taken the last of the furniture going to Wyoming, and Catherine had sent Ole Bill to collect the three small beds that they had used last night.

Catherine had insisted on treating everyone to breakfast. The twins were noisy, but it was the good noise of happy children. Between the squeals and giggles, the children showed off their new cat, and Zadie quickly made some sketches of the little orange tabby. As they left, Catherine handed them a basket filled with food for their trip. The only thing they had to do now was wait.

Ole Bill came to collect Zadie, her mom, and Abilene, along with their trunks, to take them to the train station. Zadie had sent a telegram to Duncan, alerting him to retrieve her in Laramie along with three large trunks on November 11. She refused to ever take that stagecoach again. Then she prayed he'd get the telegram before she arrived. But it was after she sent it that she realized she never said that she was bringing her mother and Abilene.

***

Duncan wrapped his scarf over his lower face and headed for the barn. Wind whipped around him and cut like a dozen knives into his skin. He strained to pull the door open and then strained to keep the door from slamming closed. The door opened behind him and he realized Five Paws had followed him.

"It cold. Wind come too fast."

Duncan nodded. "Do you think it will bring more snow?"

"These winds always bring snow, but it too soon for such weather."

"I wanted to go to town today and see if there is mail from Zadie."

"You think she come back here?"

Duncan nodded. "Each letter has held promise of her return."

Five Paws rolled his lip up like a snarling dog. "White man not keep promises."

"Don't say things like that. I am white and I'm keeping my promises to you."

"You different. You not like other white men." Five Paws walked away and cocked his head.

"You hear something?"

A moment later, they both heard Dora Grace scream.

Duncan grabbed his rifle and flew out the door behind Five Paws. Two horses had Government Issue saddles, but no riders.

Five Paws had his hunting knife in his hand as he motioned for Duncan to take the back door of the cabin.

Duncan stepped through the door and

instantly spotted two young men in his kitchen.

Dora Grace was cowered in a corner.

"What are you doing here?"

"Two things. You got Indians living here."

"This is my land and I can allow whoever I want on it. I can also remove trespassers." Duncan raised his rifle.

"No need to get upset. You are Duncan Lorde."

Duncan nodded.

"We only need to know who they are, from what tribe, and how many you have here. The government likes to see them all accounted for and living like civilized people." From a pocket inside his coat, the man pulled out a book and another piece of paper. "Here. It's the second thing. This telegram came for you, and we said we'd bring it since we were headed here this morning."

Duncan took the piece of paper and

unfolded it.

ARRIVE LARAMIE NOV 11 [STOP]
3 LARGE TRUNKS [STOP] NO
STAGECOACH [STOP] ZADIE [STOP]

Duncan could feel his blood draining towards his feet. "It's Zadie. She's coming to Laramie today and wants me to come get her with the buckboard."

The older of the two young men asked, "In this weather?"

Duncan swallowed. "Yes."

"Mr. Lorde, you might outrun this storm on the way down but you won't get back here anytime soon."

"What about the two of you?"

"We're going to try to make it to Sheridan. There's a boarding house there."

Duncan looked at Five Paws. It was as though the Indian could read minds and shook his head. Duncan motioned with his thumb towards the house and Five Paws shrugged.

"Officers, I have a house. I'm about to bring my bride to it, but there's no furniture actually in there because I haven't moved anything into it, but you are welcome to use it if you don't mess it up."

"You mean the furniture is here, but not in the house?"

"It's in crates in the house."

The two men looked at each other and the younger one shrugged.

The older one chuckled. "You go grab your mail-order bride and we'll uncrate everything as payment for keeping us out of this storm."

"She's not mail order. Our fathers were best friends."

The men chuckled. "Heard that one before. Just wait until she arrives."

Duncan didn't feel like arguing with them. "Five Paws will show you to the house. Stay away from his wife, Dora Grace, or he'll kill you."

"We need some information on them," the younger man said.

"Five Paws speaks English." Duncan walked out of the cabin. "Take care of the animals. I'll be back as soon as I can."

***

The train came to a screeching halt and Zadie looked out the window. The land was flat, white, and barren. Falling snow meant she couldn't see far. She couldn't tell what stopped them this time, but she had a feeling it had something to do with the snow. They had the whole car to themselves and she didn't mind being alone with her mom and Abilene. There was another family that was supposed to ride with them on this part of the trip, but when the mother discovered Abilene was staying in the car, the mother had refused to board and had some choice words for the conductor about a darkie being in the same Pullman.

This had been the quietest leg of the trip and Zadie knew she needed it, as this was the end of her previous life. Even her mother had stopped crying.

Two men entered the car with pistols drawn. They had long hair and they were dressed like Indians complete with war paint.

Zadie couldn't help but laugh, because they looked like mummers.

The men wagged their pistols at them. "Give us your money."

Zadie glanced at her mom who had turned white and looked on the verge of passing out. Abilene was trying to fan Zadie's mother.

The men turned to Zadie who was now covering her mouth to hide her laughter. The sheer stupidity of the situation had caught her off guard and sent her into a fit of giggles. Tears were starting to run down her cheeks. Between her laughter, she managed to squeak out a few words, but they weren't in English. As she had taught Dora Grace a few words, Dora Grace had taught Zadie.

"Give us your money!"

"I already told you." Zadie rolled her eyes at them. "Don't you know your own language? My mother is a widow, and I spent the last of our money on train tickets. I have a man in Laramie waiting to marry me." Then she told them where the door was in the language Dora Grace had used.

She knew the men were anything but Indians.

"What's in those trunks?"

She shrugged. "Mostly clothes."

"Open them."

She purposely opened her mother's trunk, knowing her mother's parasol was next to her father's shotgun. She grabbed the parasol, opening it as she grabbed her father's shotgun. "There's not much here to interest anyone other than a lady."

She kicked the trunk with one foot to make the lid fall as she cocked the gun and closed the parasol around the gun. She quickly prayed that she had managed to cover the sound of the hammer being drawn back.

"What was that?" The one man looked at the other.

Zadie laughed. "There's nothing here but widow's weeds. I already told you. We don't have anything. Come see for yourself."

Duncan's words ran through her mind. But sometimes you only have two choices. Kill or be killed. That's when you will shoot.

The men stepped towards her, and Zadie said a quick prayer. Let's see if I can hit the side of the barn, Duncan. As they stepped a little closer, she raised the disguised gun and pulled the trigger.

Her mother passed out, and Abilene screamed. Zadie tried not to vomit as her stomach contents rose into her throat. She had shot them both in the face. Certain she had blinded the one; she watched the other fall to the floor.

"Abilene, help me! We've got to get their coats off."

"Why? Are you daft?"

"No. They will not survive in the cold without coats." She leaned down and felt the neck of the one man on the floor. "He doesn't have long to live." She whipped his coat off and dragged his body out of the car. Positioned by the steps, she used her foot to push him, and then watched his crumpled body roll down into the snow.

But Abilene was having a more difficult time with the man who was blinded, even though she'd managed to take his gun. When he grabbed Abilene, Zadie snatched a pair of her mother's scissors from the trunk and sliced the man's arm. Blood spurted, telling her she'd hit a vital spot. A moment later, they managed to get him out of the train's car before he collapsed.

They stood on the metal platform, and Abilene grunted as they pushed the limp body into the snow.

Zadie waited, knowing there were probably more robbers. She tossed an old skirt at Abilene. "Wrap it around your arm and pretend you are wounded. There's too much blood here."

Zadie then hid the robbers' coats behind the trunks. She looked over at her mother who had fainted. Oh, Momma, stay that way. She reloaded the gun, cocked it, and waited. She didn't have long to wait before another man walked into the car. He was wearing a conductor's jacket and cap, but his so-called war paint remained near his hairline.

"Is everything fine here?"

Zadie shook her head and in her most controlled voice said, "No, they shot my momma and my nanny before running out the back door."

Zadie looked at the man's riding boots, knowing conductors wore shoes. The man stepped closer to Zadie. She took a breath before squeezing the trigger.

The man rocked as his hand flew to his neck. Between his fingers, blood pulsed out as if being forced by a strong pump. "Abilene, push him from the car. He'll never survive."

Zadie watched as he collapsed, but Abilene managed to roll him down to the snow.

"Do you think that's all of them?"

Zadie shook her head. "No way to tell."

They sat and waited for over an hour. Zadie's momma went from tears to silence and back to tears again. Abilene did everything she could to soothe the woman. Soon there was noise and people shouting. People walked through the snow, and decided the three men were dead. There was more shouting, more people gathering outside, and then the dead men were returned to the train.

Zadie began to shake as she put the gun and her mother's ruined parasol in the trunk and closed the lid. Abilene was dabbing cool water from the train's ewer on Zadie's momma. Abilene was covered in blood from the men, but when Zadie looked down at her own hands and dress, her world turned gray and vanished.

***

On a good day, it was a full day's drive to Laramie. This was not a good day. Duncan had brought blankets for himself and Zadie, but also for his mule. Carrying enough supplies, including firewood, to last him for several days, Duncan figured he was ahead of the snow, and he hoped to stay that way.

He reached behind him and felt for the paper that contained some jerky. Once found, he stuck a piece in his mouth. Dora Grace had just finished drying it. Tasty and chewy, it was filling.

He didn't want to stop. He pushed onwards. Light was beginning to dwindle, but Laramie was still far away. Snow began to fall. Big flakes swirled through the air. "Come on, Nellie, we've got to get there while we can still find the road."

He lightly slapped the reins to let his mule know she could pick up speed, and she did. It was as if she wanted to get out of the snow, too. "That's a girl! Let's get Zadie."

The mule picked up more speed, but Duncan wondered if he would have been better off bringing Rocky, except Rocky would not be as capable of pulling a heavy load. Duncan mumbled to himself, "That horse adores her."

Snow turned to sleet. It hit the back of Duncan's neck, taking him by surprise and making him inhale. He turned his collar up and repositioned his hat on his head. A few minutes later, he tucked the reins between his knees as he tied his bandana over his nose and mouth, and then fished in his pockets for the extra pair of gloves that would go over his wool ones. Now the only bit of skin showing was around his eyes.

Wearing fur-lined leather pants and a jacket, he knew he looked like a trapper, but he didn't care. The clothes kept him warm and he was grateful to Dora Grace for making them. He needed to reach Zadie. *Zadie, my Zadie, I've missed you.*

The sleet switched back to snow and continued to whirl around him. His world was white, and he couldn't see anything more than a few feet away. *Please, let me get there.* He tsked once and slapped the reins. "Come on, ole girl. We have to retrieve Zadie."

***

Zadie followed a lawman to a house where she was introduced to the sheriff's wife.

"This here is Mrs. Bateman."

Zadie didn't even have the energy left to smile. She looked at her blood-covered hands and shook her head.

"She's not under arrest, but we don't want her running off until we've gotten her statement."

Zadie's mother spoke. "Pleased to meet you, Mrs. Bateman. I'm Mrs. Larkford. This is Abilene, and my daughter, Zadie. We do appreciate you allowing us to clean up after the ordeal we experienced."

"Yes. Please come in. My kitchen is warm and you'll be able to clean up in there." She turned to the lawman. "Now, Bill, you just wait in the parlor until we're done. There's no reason for a man to watch a woman bathe. That's just not proper."

Zadie's mom physically pushed Zadie to follow the sheriff's wife through the house and into the kitchen. Zadie watched as the woman stoked the fire in the stove and fixed a large basin of warm water.

Abilene took the cloth that Zadie had been offered and immediately washed her own arms and face, then rinsed the cloth. "I can't wash Zadie when I'm covered in blood, too."

Zadie's mom nodded as Abilene removed Zadie's dress.

Abilene began washing Zadie. Zadie simply closed her eyes and allowed Abilene to take control. It was like being a child again, as it had been years since she'd had Abilene's help. The sensation of the warm wet cloth being gently rubbed over Zadie's skin was comforting, and after what she'd been through, she needed to be wrapped in the soothing reassurance that her nanny provided.

"That's much better. My baby girl looks almost as good as new. We don't want to wash your hair and have you going into this cold weather. But I managed to wipe the worst away."

Zadie wanted to say thank you, wanted to say something, but words didn't form in her mouth. It was as though she'd forgotten how to make them. Zadie stepped into her charcoal-gray dress with the pale purple trim. The lavender color reminded her of the fall-blooming asters that often popped up in a field or along a fence line. She stood still as Abilene buttoned her dress.

Abilene took Zadie's hair down, brushed it, and braided it, making a bun with the braid. A few hairpins later, Mrs. Bateman escorted Zadie to a table, handed her a hot cup of tea, and a sweet treat called scones. Her mother joined her wearing a clean dress as well, and Abilene took her tea as she stood by the stove. At home, she would have joined them, but Abilene knew not everyone was accepting of the help being treated like family.

Zadie's mom put down her cup. "Are you ready to give your statement to the sheriff, Zadie?"

Zadie shook her head.

Abilene stepped forward. "Zadie May Larkford. I'm going to tell you something." Abilene shook her finger in Zadie's face. "The cat didn't steal your tongue. You are going to tell that sheriff everything you did and how you saved our lives." Abilene raised her eyebrows. "If you don't, you are going to be wearing my handprint, because you will never be too old for me to spank!"

Zadie swallowed the lump in her throat and managed a meek reply, "Yes, ma'am."

Three hours later, Zadie, her mother, and Abilene, approached the train. A conductor escorted them to a different car and Zadie was grateful that she didn't have to look at the bloodied Pullman that had brought them this far. As Zadie boarded, the passengers began to cheer and clap.

Another conductor approached Zadie. "Miz Larkford, the people on this train decided to take a collection for you. They heard it was you who killed those men, and they are grateful for what you did. Because of you, everyone got their jewelry and money back."

Zadie took the proffered hankie that had been made into a pouch. "Please tell everyone this is much appreciated. My mother is a widow."

She dropped the pouch of money into her pocket. It was heavy but she had no idea if it was filled with pennies or silver dollars.

***

Duncan could barely see the road as he made his way towards Laramie. Several times, he thought about giving up and making a campfire, but he worried about Zadie coming into town alone and maybe without enough money for a hotel room, especially after what she had said about her mother's financial situation.

It had been dark for hours, but the accumulation of snow had been minimal. This was a dry snow and it seemed most of it was blowing through the air instead of piling on the ground. At least he could still find the ruts in the road.

"Okay, Nellie. I need a break. I can barely feel my feet and nature is calling me." He reined his mule to a halt. Carefully he stood and stepped from the wagon. He'd heard of people breaking bones when they couldn't feel their feet and he didn't want to do that. He relieved himself and then rummaged for something to eat. The jerky had made him thirsty and the water in his canteen had frozen solid. He took a scoop of snow knowing it might help his thirst but make him feel colder, as his body would have to work to warm the snow. He thought about being home in Edenton, North Carolina, and his father's warning about not drinking the brackish water that filled the rivers. At least it's not salt water.

He swung his arms and began to lift his knees in an attempt to warm his body. Then he checked Nellie's hooves. She was fine, so he returned to his seat on the buckboard. "Let's go, Nellie."

It had to have been an hour later when he knew he was approaching Laramie. It still took him time to get into the town. Not seeing the train or any signs of Zadie, he took Nellie to the livery.

"Where's a hotel that won't cost six week's pay in this town?"

The man at the livery didn't even look up as he answered, "Go past the big hotel and there's a small one another block down. You don't get much. But the big hotel will get you a meal tonight and breakfast tomorrow morning. It's much nicer. That little hotel can get rowdy with all the cowboys we've got in town tonight."

"Thanks." Duncan walked to the big hotel, and as he did, he heard the whistle of a distant train. Zadie isn't going to stay in some cowboy establishment. But, if she has already arrived, would she have enough money for a real hotel?

Duncan entered the hotel. It was a beauty, with gold and crystal decorations and velvet seating. He stepped up to the counter and rang the bell. As he waited, he began to unbutton his jacket.

A man appeared. "Yes, sir. What can I do for you?"

"Two things. Is Miss Zadie Larkford

here? And can I get a small room with a meal tonight and breakfast in the morning?"

The train whistle blew again.

The man behind the counter looked at his pocket watch. "That train should have been here seven hours ago. Word came through that they were robbed." The man opened his registration book. "The cheapest room I've got left is six dollars for the night and I can give you meals with it."

Duncan sucked in his breath and held it. He was hungry and cold. "Fine. I'll take it."

"No one here by the name of Larkford." The man played with his handlebar mustache.

"Thanks. Any other places in town where she might have stayed?"

"Not really."

***

Zadie didn't have far to ride, but it was pitch dark as the train pulled into Laramie. Snow covered everything. Zadie looked around, but she could barely see the street and she didn't see anyone waiting for her. Her heart fell into her stomach. Had Duncan received her telegram?

***

Duncan nodded and took the key. He was halfway to his room when the train's whistle and the clerk's words meshed in his mind. Zadie!

He dropped his bags in his room and flew to the door of the hotel. He shoved it open and listened to it bang behind him as he stepped into the icy cold air. "Zadie! Zadie!"

He ran towards the train station. Through the dense white cloud of snow, he saw a cluster of people. "Zadie!"

"Duncan?"

She ran to him and he picked her up, spinning her around in his arms as his lips crashed into hers. "You really are back."

"Of course I'm back." She ran her fingers through his beard. "This tickles."

"It keeps me warmer when tending the animals. I told you; it's cold out here."

She looked at him, and he realized how tall she was, almost equaling him in height. His lips found hers and she wrapped her arms around him and held him tight. When he broke the kiss, he started to turn her to the hotel.

"No, wait. I'm not alone." She turned around and faced the train station. "This is my mother and Abilene."

You brought your mother? Duncan tried to let that revelation sink into his mind.

"Oh, and I shot and killed three men."

Certainly this was some sort of a dream. He stood riveted in place while trying to make sense of her last few sentences. His head pounded. "You brought your mother and Abilene, and you've killed three men?"

He was as lost as the snow that drifted around him. Has my wish for a wife made me lose my senses? I can't afford a maid, a mother-in-law, and a wife. I can barely survive. Then he looked at Zadie and his heart melted. He knew he would do anything to keep her by his side.

"Pleased to meet you, Mrs. Larkford." He turned to Abilene. "Zadie's said you are like family to her."

Wind, carrying snow, whipped around them, and Duncan knew the women needed to be in the warmth of the hotel. "There's the hotel. We can talk more in there."

10

"Our trunks?" Zadie asked.

"I'll ask at the hotel if someone will bring them." Duncan offered his arms to Mrs. Larkford and Abilene. "I don't want anyone to lose her footing in this snow. Zadie, please allow me to escort your mother and Abilene. I'm certain you are more sure-footed. But be careful, there are patches of ice under this snow."

They entered the hotel and Duncan rang the bell. The man with the handlebar mustache stepped to the counter with a distinct frown.

"What now?"

"I need a three-bedroom suite with a toilet and bath."

The man looked at the three women. "We don't have rooms for niggers."

Duncan remembered his father punching a man in the mouth for calling one of his fishermen a nigger. His father had taught Duncan that all men were men and were to be respected no matter what their color. If they did a man's job, they were to be paid a man's wage. And from the look on Zadie's face, he knew she was about to explode. He practically smacked her on the back to keep her mouth shut.

"You will not separate these women from Abilene. Mrs. Larkford has just lost her husband, the famous Dr. Gregory Larkford of Franklin, Virginia. He was a prominent physician in the medical society and a beloved doctor by his patients in Virginia. You will find them a room, and I do not want to hear you refer to their dear Abilene by any name other than ma'am. She will take all her meals with them and be treated as family." Duncan raised his eyebrows. "Do you understand or do I need to help you comprehend the gravity of this situation?"

"The Dr. Gregory Larkford of Virginia?"

Duncan nodded, knowing the man before him had no idea who the small town doctor really was.

"Um, yes. We have a room for them. I'm so sorry. I understand that the train you were traveling on was robbed."

Zadie spoke up, "Yes. I shot them when they threatened my mother and Abilene." She looked at Duncan. "He taught me to use a gun the last time I was in Wyoming."

"I heard it was a woman who saved the passengers. I had no idea it was such a lady."

Zadie stood a little straighter. "I did what I

had to do. Being a lady had nothing to do with it. Our room please."

The man quickly produced a key. "Room 316. I'm certain you will find it satisfactory. May I have the kitchen offer you some food?"

Duncan spoke up. "Yes. Please send a menu to the room, and we need someone to retrieve their trunks on the platform of the train station. I will be taking my meals with them."

Duncan snatched the key.

"That will be fourteen dollars."

Duncan smiled. "And it includes meals and an extra night or two if we need it."

The man began to protest, but Duncan cut him off. "You certainly would not want to offend the widow of Dr. Larkford, or his daughter who saved the train from a robbery."

Duncan reached into his pouch and paid the man. Then he escorted the women to their room. A few minutes later, their trunks arrived and so did the menu.

Realizing as they ate their late meal that Zadie wasn't quite herself, he figured she was still in shock, and knew that sleep would be the best thing for her. "I'll see everyone tomorrow morning." He turned to Zadie. "I'm really proud of you."

Zadie looked up and tears filled her eyes.

Was her fierce independence a mask that hid an overly sensitive female?

***

Two days later, Duncan, Abilene, Zadie, and her mother made the journey to Duncan's ranch. The snow had stopped, but what was on the ground was not enough to warrant using runners on the buckboard. The bitter cold would make the trip grueling. Duncan had made certain they had plenty of blankets, but Abilene pulled more from their trunks. Zadie's mom sat up front with Duncan, and Zadie sat with Abilene in the bed of the buckboard, which was not as comfortable.

Zadie felt sorry for Abilene and did everything she could to make the trip as tolerable as possible for the older woman. But the trip was long and bumpy. Light was beginning to fade as they neared Creed's Crossing, and they only had another hour to go before they would make it to the ranch.

"I thought you said your ranch was up ahead?" her mother asked.

"It won't be long now." Duncan lightly slapped the mule's reins.

Zadie turned to Duncan. "Do you think Dora Grace will have dinner ready for us?"

"No. She has no way of knowing when we will arrive or that there are so many of us. Maybe you can give her a hand and help her fix food."

Zadie's heart fell into her hungry stomach. "Where are we all going to sleep?"

Duncan laughed. "With luck, in the house. It may not be what you envisioned, but it will be enough for tonight. We can rearrange the furniture tomorrow."

"Not the cabin?"

"I'll sleep in the cabin unless you want me in the house. I'd be honored to share your bed."

Zadie caught him giving her mother a little nudge and a wink. She laughed. "I've killed three men, what's one more?"

"Zadie!" Mrs. Larkford turned to her daughter. "You've told me a dozen times that Duncan is a gentleman. I do believe he was merely teasing you."

Duncan laughed and the sound rolled over Zadie like a warm blanket.

"You've already warned me what will happen if the stoves go out through the night.

Maybe it would be best if you stay in the house with us. But certainly you can find your own room."

Duncan chuckled. "Any room with you in it will be fine."

"Duncan Lorde! How dare you? And in front of Abilene and my momma!"

Zadie caught him winking at her mother again.

"Well, you were planning on marrying me, were you not? So what difference does a few days matter?"

Zadie's ire rose in her, and she huffed at his tease. "You have no sense of decorum!"

"That's right, I don't. I've waited for months for you and now you are here. How long do you expect me to pretend I don't want you sleeping in my bed?"

Zadie made a throaty sound that showed her displeasure.

Duncan chuckled.

Abilene laughed. "Oh, Zadie. What are you waiting for? You've kept him on strings for ages."

Anger whipped through Zadie like a wildfire. "No one is going to force me into marriage! I don't find any of this funny."

***

Duncan could feel the worry in the back of his neck. He had no idea how much furniture Zadie had sent or what he was walking into, and he had no idea if Zadie's family would eat anything that Dora Grace had fixed. Plus Zadie's comments weren't exactly what he'd wanted to hear. He drove past the house and on to the cabin. "Please introduce your family to Five Paws and Dora Grace while I take care of the trunks and Nellie."

He helped the women from the buckboard and all three stood with their hands on their lower backs as if they were afraid that the few steps to the cabin might snap their cold bodies in half. He felt sorry for Abilene, for he would have referred to her as an old lady, yet she never once complained during the entire trip. Nellie was tired, but she took him to the house and waited patiently as he unloaded the heavy trunks. He went to the kitchen, started a fire in the stove, and lit the coal stoves. At least the house would be warm for them. Then he headed to the barn. He knew he had left Five Paws with a difficult task of caring for the animals when he'd had the buckboard. But he could see where they had plenty of hay and a few head were at the troughs.

If he could survive this evening, he was certain things would improve. He looked towards the house and could see the smoke rising from the chimneys. It was a good sign.

As he entered the cabin, he could hear Dora Grace and Five Paws. Whatever they were saying wasn't positive from their tone. Abilene was in the kitchen. Mrs. Larkford was sitting in a chair at the table and Zadie was missing. His head throbbed. He strode to the kitchen, determined to sort out whatever was happening.

***

Abilene had thrown up her hands and chased Dora Grace from the kitchen when she saw what she was doing to the meat. That sent Dora Grace into a panic, which upset Five Paws. Zadie had tried to intervene and explain that Abilene was the family cook. But Dora Grace must have felt as though her position had been usurped.

Zadie was out of patience with everyone

being upset over the silliest things. She walked out the back door and went to the house, expecting to find Duncan there. Instead, it was empty. Someone had placed furniture in the rooms, but most of it was not where she wanted it. As she looked around, she wondered why she had sent some of it. It's our furniture, and once I get it in place, it will feel more like home.

She lit a candle and went upstairs. The bedroom furniture was mixed and the beds were not in the rooms where she had pictured them, but someone had put linens on each of them. That would save them some time this evening. Whoever made up the beds, made them tight. The upstairs was almost warm, and the bathing room was quite toasty with its pretty, blue and white-painted tile stove. She tried all of the spigots, two for the sink and two for the tub, and discovered running hot and cold water. The toilet had a high tank and a pull chain to flush the bowl clean. Duncan hadn't spared any expense when it came to the bathing room.

As she walked down the hall, she noticed the soft glow from her candle on the wall. Duncan had created a beautiful home. It might not be grand in size, but it was charming. She sat on the steps and thought about his house. She would do all that she could to make it into a home. Men want to be proud of their home.

"Zadie, are you here?"

The sound of Duncan's voice made her smile. "Yes, I'm sitting on the back stairs."

He rounded the corner and took the steps two at a time. "What are you doing? It's suppertime, and it seems as though everyone in the cabin is upset."

She shrugged. "I know, and I needed some time alone. I don't like when everyone fails to act civilly towards each other. I'm sure it's from traveling and all the recent events. It's as though the world is closing in and I needed to be by myself."

Duncan nodded and then smiled. "Do you like the house?"

"Yes. It's beautiful. Look how the light plays on the walls."

"I know. I noticed that, too. They told me the man who did all the plastering was good. I like the way it turned out." He held out his hand to her.

She smiled as she placed her hand into his.

"Are you having any second thoughts about killing those men?"

"Yes, and no. I think about it, but then I remember you saying that I will kill, when it's kill or be killed."

"I almost can't believe that you managed to hit anyone."

"My father's gun was loaded with fowl shot for hunting ducks. The men were close and I aimed for their abdomens."

Duncan laughed. "That's my Zadie. I'm very proud of you." He pulled her to her feet. "Shall we return to the cabin for our meal?"

She nodded. "May we start fixing the rooms tomorrow? I want everything in its proper place."

"Allow me to check the herd first, then I'll have Five Paws help me with the furniture."

"You asked about killing those men. My father was dedicated to saving lives, and in a matter of minutes I ended three lives." She picked up the candle and handed it to Duncan.

Duncan chuckled. "I'm willing to bet, from what you've said about your father, that your father would have killed anyone who threatened his little girl, wife, or Abilene. You did the right thing."

"Everyone acted as though I was an angel for what I'd done. But that's not the way it feels." She walked with Duncan down the stairs and to the back door

Duncan blew out the candle and left it on the table near the door. Then he helped Zadie with her coat. "That doesn't surprise me. Remember, things are different out here. You did what you needed to do, even if it wasn't pleasant."

She nodded, but something inside of her had changed. She was no longer Dr. Larkford's carefree daughter. It seemed as though her innocence had vanished in the last few months, and she didn't know the person she had become. "Duncan?"

"Yes."

"I know I shouldn't ask. But would you…before we go inside…I want to feel…Oh this is so wrong. Ignore me. I must be addled."

Duncan touched her cheek. "What do you want, my darling Zadie? Tell me."

She shook her head. How could I ever tell you that I want your arms around me and your lips on mine? Then she mumbled, "Kiss me?"

***

"Momma, no. It doesn't matter that you and Poppa always had it in Poppa's office. That's not where I want it." Zadie put her fingertips to her forehead. Her head pounded a little harder with each dispute over a piece of furniture.

Duncan tapped Zadie on her shoulder and whispered, "It's a few pieces of wood fitted together. It's not worth an argument and hurt feelings."

Between closed teeth she hissed, "Tell that to her!"

"I will."

Everyone worked through dinner and almost until suppertime. When they finally quit, Zadie went to the second floor and tossed herself across her bed. Her head was still throbbing and her entire body ached.

A soft knock made her roll over. The remaining sunlight coming through the window made her cover her eyes. "Come in."

"Are you certain?" Duncan stepped into the room.

"Oh, I thought you were Momma."

He sat on the bottom corner of her bed. "Are you ill?"

"No. But after today, I have a terrible headache. I never would have dreamed that placing furniture would be so difficult. I had visions of it being a joyful event. Instead my mother was determined to place everything exactly the way it was in Franklin."

Duncan chuckled.

His voice normally would have warmed her soul, but the added sound made her head pound even more. She touched her finger to her lips. "Whisper. Any noise makes my head hurt."

"What can I do for you? I don't want to see you like this."

"Will you bring my dinner up here? I think skipping meals didn't help."

"Meals as in plural?"

"I only had coffee this morning. And it's that..." She realized what she almost said. Her embarrassment crept up her neck and flooded her cheeks with heat.

After a moment of silence, he put his hand on her ankle. "I understand. I have sisters. It seems women often need a respite."

"I--"

"I'll bring your supper. Rest."

She felt awkward, partly because such a

conversation was considered unsuitable, and because she truly felt horrid.

Nothing is going as planned. Is this what my life will be?

***

Duncan wandered from room to room. What he thought would take him months and maybe years to accomplish had taken place in one day. His humble house was filled with beautiful furniture that would rival any of Edenton's finest. A stack of pictures had been leaned against a wall. He looked through them and realized they were all Zadie's. Not daring to attempt to hang them for her, he merely admired her work until he heard Abilene fussing at Dora Grace.

Oh, no! He could tell that Dora Grace was upset from the way she pressed her lips together. He forced a friendly smile. "Dear Abilene, I know Zadie would be upset to see you flustered like this. So please tell me how I can help you."

Abilene shook her head. "She's trying to put a fire in the oven instead of the firebox."

"She's never used this stove. She never used a stove at all until she used mine. Probably never saw a stove until she came to live with me. Can't fault her for what she doesn't know." He turned to Dora Grace, and using the words he knew of her language, he told her where the wood went. "Let Abilene show you how to cook on this stove. She taught Zadie and now will teach you. Please bring vegetables and meat for Abilene to cook." Then he watched Dora Grace walk out the door and head to the cold cellar.

Abilene started to say something and he held his palm out to her. "She understands us but can't always answer in our language. Give her a chance."

Sufficiently satisfied at smoothing the ruffled feathers of two females, he left to see what Dora Grace intended to make for dinner.

Two hours later, supper was served, and he took Zadie's to her room. She had obviously been sleeping and was happy to see her meal.

"How's your headache?"

She sat up in bed and accepted the tray of food. "Better, I think. Maybe eating will help."

She took a spoonful of the stew. "What am I eating? It tastes odd."

"Venison. I killed a deer last week."

"Oh." She ate another spoonful. "I know that a steak comes from a cow and a pig supplies our bacon, but I try not to think of how they supply it."

"I can understand that. Just don't think

about it." He couldn't help but wonder how she would survive on a ranch. "But you'll have to come to grips with the fact that I'm raising cattle as food. They aren't pets."

She nodded. "I know." Then she scrunched her face. "I really did kill those three men."

"This is the west. Your safety depends on how well you can protect yourself." He looked at his calloused hands, stained from hard work. "Not everyone out here is what you would call a good, God-fearing person...even in town. You'll learn, and you'll learn who is your friend."

As he looked towards the door of her room, he prayed her mother wasn't going to discover him sitting on the corner of her bed. There wasn't anything wrong with what he was doing, even if it didn't seem proper, but the impropriety of the situation stabbed at him.

It was one thing to joke about sharing her bed and quite another for a man to be in a woman's room. Even staying in the house with her was wrong, but he wasn't going to leave her alone to handle stoves or any situation that might arise. "You did what you had to do to protect yourself and your family. I wasn't there, but I'm proud of you."

"Thank you. Your words give me comfort." She lifted her tray and handed it to him. "No walk tonight?"

"It's a little chilly, but if that's what you want..." He stood and strolled towards the door.

She forced a tiny smile. "Eat your supper and I'll see how I feel."

He stopped in her doorway and turned back to her. The feelings inside of him rose faster than the winds of a hurricane. "Zadie..."

"Yes?"

"I love you."

Zadie watched Duncan walk away, but his words dangled in the air like a forgotten marionette. Zadie swallowed. Maybe that was all she'd ever wanted to hear. Or were they the words that she feared the most? She thought about Catherine and about several friends who had attended college with her. How many of these women had given up everything to be a wife? Is that what she wanted? Was her choice of returning to Duncan based on her mother's financial situation? Her feelings scrambled as her heart tightened into a hard ball. What do I do?

She thought about Duncan sitting on the edge of her bed as though it was the most natural thing in the world. The warmth of his hand on her blanket-covered ankle still lingered. She didn't want him to leave. She wanted him to stay, to hold her in his arms and to kiss her.

Slowly she pulled herself from the bed, washed her face, and brushed her teeth in the pretty new bathing room. She needed to talk to Duncan, but she didn't know what to say. How did she tell him her feelings? What about the feelings that she had bundled and hidden for so long? She was still holding onto the grief of losing her father. But she had feelings for Duncan, exciting, lusty feelings for him that seemed to tickle her entire body and wrap her in joy.

His hair, no longer kissed from the strong summer sun, had faded to a dark blond, and his face was covered with whiskers. Did his chest hair darken like the hair on his head? It must.

A lock curled over his forehead and she had watched him absently push it away several times while he'd been in her room. She wanted to run her fingers through his hair.

She had seen the arms of loggers. Their veins lay atop of heavy arm muscles. Duncan had those same arms and his pants grabbed at his thigh and calf muscles. She remembered seeing his bare chest. No man had ever made her feel the way she felt for him. Her breath hitched.

What am I doing? Why?

***

Duncan stood when Zadie entered the parlor.

"Excuse me, Momma. Duncan offered to take me for a walk. I thought the fresh air would help me."

Zadie's mom nodded.

Abilene shook her head as though she didn't believe a word Zadie said. "Any excuse to be alone?"

"Please excuse us," Duncan offered in

the direction of the two older women, and then turned back to Zadie. "You will need your warmest coat."

Zadie nodded.

He helped her into her coat and then put on his. He opened the front door. As they stepped out, a slight breeze caught them, and he listened to her catch her breath in the bitter cold. "Are you certain you want to walk?"

"Not really. Abilene said it. I only wanted to be alone with you."

He took her hand and went to the barn. It wasn't really any warmer in there, but at least they weren't where the wind would slice them like an artic knife. He created a sitting area for them, but Zadie wouldn't sit.

"You said something to me... Do you mean it?"

"I've never said anything to you that I didn't mean." He sat on a barrel that had once held nails for his house. "Zadie, I've reached a point in my life where I knew I was ready to settle down and have a family. I wanted someone to share my life with me."

His heart beat in his chest at twice its normal speed. "Your letters made me laugh. I hadn't laughed since I came here. Nor did I realize how much I'd missed all those lighter feelings in life." He looked at his hands and then at the walls around him. "My ranch is everything, and all I did was work towards making it a success, but someplace along the way, I'd forgotten about having fun. Your banter was like sunshine in my otherwise clouded life."

"You said you loved me."

"Oh. Zadie... I prayed for a woman who would make my life worth living. I prayed that she'd be easy on my eyes, and my prayers were answered a hundred times over. The woman who came to me was beyond my dreams." He looked at her and smiled. "She has a beautiful dark mane of hair and eyes that match it. She's intelligent and the most amazing artist. I never dreamed she would be so wonderful."

"But can you accept that she will never be some meek little wife?"

He chuckled. "Oh, those women are easy to obtain - women who will do anything to have a man marry them." He stood and went to her. "That's not what I wanted. A mail order bride would have assured that. I wanted a woman who would love me, not because I have a ranch, but because she found pleasure in the things that I do." I want more, Zadie, but are you willing to give it to me? "I'm not certain how to say this... I want you to love me as much as I love you."

She looked directly at him, and he felt

the intensity of her stare.

"It's beautiful here. But, I will always love home. I will miss the egrets and the heron that fish in our waters."

"And the taste of fresh oysters?"

"Yes." Her tongue darted between her lips.

"It's different here. I hated being on the water with my brothers. I hated the stench of the herring packinghouse."

"And ranching?"

"It's different, but in a sense...maybe it's the same. My father said, when he started, he only had dreams. And that's all I have."

"I believe you have more than dreams. Look at your house. A man with only dreams would not have been able to accomplish this."

"I built it for you." He leaned towards her, and she responded by putting her hands on his upper arms. Their faces were only inches apart, and her breath wafted over his face. The sweet scent of her sent his body places it had never been. "Yes, Zadie, for you. I love you."

His lips found hers, and his eyes closed. She was everything he wanted, but what did she want? Could he provide it, or would she always be reaching for something he couldn't obtain or couldn't afford?

11

Zadie melted at Duncan's intimate touch. His kiss was what she wanted. It was anything but proper, and right now, she didn't want to follow convention. She wanted Duncan to sweep her away on some sort of tide - wanted to know him as a woman knows a man.

He broke his kiss from her. "I should not have done that."

She ran her hands over her cheeks. His beard tickled and it was a delicious feeling, masculine and exciting. "Why did you stop?"

"Because…"

"I want you, Duncan."

He raised his eyebrows. "Want and love are two different things."

Zadie grinned at him. "For a woman to truly want a man, she must love him. Otherwise, she is nothing more than a cat that caterwauls in the night air. My desire comes from deep within me. It is built upon a deep friendship and trust."

She stepped away from him and went to Rocky's stall. The horse lifted his head to her and she ran her hand from his forehead to his muzzle. He bunted her hand as though looking for a treat. "Duncan, I had many suitors, but they were not who I wanted. I frustrated my family, because they did not understand my feelings. Even now, my mother wonders why we are not married."

"I wonder why we are not married."

Duncan stood behind her and placed his hands on her shoulders. "What do I need to do to convince you to marry me? What will it take?"

She moved from his touch. "For me to be certain that this is what I truly want..." She turned, looked into his eyes, and saw his passion. Digging through her mind for the words to explain it to him would not be easy, for she was still feeling some confusion within herself. "It is a feeling inside of me. Up until a few months ago, I didn't have to worry about another person. I only had to please myself, and I did. I painted when and what I wanted. I wasn't asking for gemstones, only an occasional tube of paint or an occasional pair of shoes or dress. There was always money for such items."

"If that is all you want; I should always have a little cash for such expenses. But maybe it is best if you ask before you spend."

She turned back to Rocky and scratched under his chin. "It's more than a few dollars. When I was little, Catherine and I played together all the time. She wanted to play with her dolls, and I wanted to catch frogs."

"Nothing wrong with doing either one. I liked catching frogs."

She shook her head at him. "That's not it. From the time Catherine was eleven, she'd follow John around and make eyes at him. At thirteen, he finally noticed her. They've been together ever since. But maybe I'm still looking for frogs to catch."

"Maybe I don't understand."

Heaving a big sigh, she continued, "I've watched Catherine since I've returned home from college. She married and had the twins, but everything came with a huge price. She's paying the price with her being. She's lost herself in her marriage."

"I really don't understand. If she wanted to be married to John, and now she is, then why is that a problem?"

She walked away from Rocky and from Duncan. "Because Catherine no longer is herself. She's John's wife, and the mother of the twins. She is not Catherine. She only follows whatever John says." She lifted her arms from her sides and stretched out her hands and fingers. "I don't want to give up who I am. I don't want to give up my little bit of independence and give you the money my father left for us. I don't want it taken away from me. I want to be able to go frog hunting and not be chained to the stove or washtub."

"Or even to me?"

She spun on her heel and faced him. "Or even to you. Do you want to be chained to me? Do you want me telling you when you are allowed to walk out the door, or how far to go?"

"I see what you are saying. And when you first came here, I was afraid to have you wander off." He nodded his head. "I still am. But I didn't tell you that you were not allowed. I told you that you first had to learn to protect yourself. I still mean that. You don't go anywhere without a gun. If I tell you to stay away from certain areas, I'm telling you that for your own protection." He narrowed his eyes and stared hard at her. "When you were little, you were taught not to play with matches. As an adult, you know why. I will do what I must to protect my woman - the women in my life, being you've given me two more."

"I'm sorry. But what else could I do with Momma and Abilene? I'd be running back and forth to Franklin if I had not brought them here with me."

"You did what you had to do." He shrugged. "Maybe having them here will allow you to go frog hunting and not be chained to the stove. Forgive me ... I thought women wanted to take care of their husbands just as men want to take care of their wives."

She sat on the wooden barrel, propping her elbow on her knee and her chin on her hand. "I'm not saying I don't want a husband or to do things for him. How do I say this?" She could feel the tears starting to slide down her cheeks and she hated that he'd so plainly seen her frustration. "How do I tell you that I don't want to lose me, the person that I am, because I've married?"

Duncan pulled her to her feet, wiped her tears with his thumbs, and smiled at her. "I don't ever want to lose that feisty woman that you are. Nor do I ever want her to stop painting or give up all those things that make her who she is. I'm in love with that woman."

She raised her eyebrows. "And what

about those dozen children?"

"What about them? The sooner we start on them, the better. It is awfully cold sleeping alone."

***

Duncan had Zadie laughing as they returned to the house. He struck a match and lit the lantern he kept by the door. "Let me show you how to stoke the stove for the night."

He added a log to the kitchen stove and when he was certain it had caught, he showed her how to turn the dials so that it would burn slowly, giving them heat through the night and plenty of embers for morning. Then he showed her his little secret. A small door through the side of the house that gave him access to the coal he had purchased. "Here's the shovel. Put enough coal in here for the stove upstairs." He used the small shovel and filled the coal bucket. "This is plenty." He wiped his hand on a rag. "Try not to handle the actual coal. It's very black, and I'm sure you don't want coal dust on your clothes." He caught how she rolled her eyes at him. "I don't know how much you know about coal."

"I know. It's what we used to heat the house in Franklin."

"Good." He handed her the lantern. "In the future, this chore can be done early in the day." He watched to see if she was going to make another face, but she didn't. "Then the coal is handy before you go to bed. Would you like to hold the lantern?"

He carried the pail to the upstairs room that contained the bath. When he opened the door to the stove in that room, he realized someone had already added enough coal to last through the night. Must have been Abilene.

"Obviously, the stove has been stoked."

He carefully emptied the pail of coal into a fancy metal urn that matched the stove. "First thing in the morning, you add more coal because you might not have much hot water until this stove reheats. I brought enough upstairs for tonight and tomorrow morning. Coal burns very hot. Be careful."

Zadie nodded. "We had coal at school. We took turns stoking the old stoves. That is one of the reasons I worried about my mother and Abilene. I know what it is like to use coal."

He left the pail in the corner of the room. "I'll take the bucket downstairs tomorrow morning."

Zadie pressed her lips together. "Give me time, Duncan. I'll tell you yes when I'm ready."

He walked her to her room in the front of the house. He had wanted to have the large room at the back of the house where he could keep an eye on the barn, but Zadie's mother had that room and the room across the hall was given to Abilene.

Zadie's explanation was that she'd always had the front room at her house in Franklin, and Abilene had always had the small, back room across from Zadie's parents. And as frazzled as everyone was, he wasn't going to demand that back room. He'd survive.

As Zadie's hand touched the doorknob of her bedroom door, she turned, and faced him. "Thank you for everything."

He didn't want to pressure her or make her feel uncomfortable, but he was determined to make certain she knew his feelings. "You are welcome. I'm glad you returned to Creed's Crossing, because I wanted you here with me."

He slipped one hand behind her neck and pulled her close to him. Then he lightly kissed her on the lips. "Goodnight, my darling Zadie."

He entered his small room and looked

across the land that went to the road. Hayricks normally dotted his view like dark sentries, but tonight's clouds obscured the moon and any light that it might have cast across his fields. Everything was black.

He went to the bed, folded back the elegant quilt that had been placed on his bed, and sat on the edge of the mattress. This was not the bed that he had made for the cabin, but an expensive one Zadie had sent from back east.

He lifted his right foot to the opposite knee and removed the boot. Then he repeated the movement to remove his left boot. He stood as he unfastened the mining overalls made from a heavy twill fabric called denim. It was warm and sturdy. The green and red flannel shirt with its long tails kept him warm. He undid the shirt's three buttons and pulled the flannel over his head. Folding his clothes, he made a neat pile at the foot of his bed. He wanted to smell fresh for Zadie, but he also didn't want to create more work for her. He lifted each arm and sniffed at his armpits. He smelled like a man, but he didn't smell like old fish or manure. He'd bathe in the morning.

Satisfied, he climbed into bed and stared at the ceiling. There was something wrong, and he could feel it clear to his bones. He slid out of bed and checked the stoves. He wandered through each unoccupied room, looking out windows. All seemed quiet, but the feeling inside of him wouldn't go away. He redressed and went to the barn. Nellie, Rocky, and Five Paws' horse were fine. He stood by his fenced fields and looked across the pasture at his livestock. All was well.

Walking back to the house, he noticed there was a small light in the kitchen. Before he was near the porch he realized that Zadie was watching him through the window.

She held the door open for him. "Is something wrong?"

He shook his head. "I couldn't sleep, so I decided to do a quick check on the ranch." He smiled at her. "Go back to bed. All is well."

"Are you certain? This is not like you."

"Yes. Everything is fine. Only sleep has eluded me." He followed Zadie upstairs and went to his room. He undressed again and climbed between the sheets, under the heavy wool blanket and the warm quilt.

He said his prayers, the ones he usually never finished before sleep overtook him. When he was done, he stared at the ceiling, praying for sleep and peace of mind. But neither one would come to him.

***

Duncan bolted upright. It sounded like distance thunder. He heard Five Paws' shouts, but not what he said. Duncan couldn't seem to dress fast enough and was still fastening buttons as he tore down the stairs. He grabbed his coat, scarf, hat, and gun belt as he dashed out the back door. Now he could tell what Five Paws was shouting. It was the Lakota word for dog and that made no sense. But his livestock had stampeded. Five Paws took off on his horse with a rifle down his back.

Duncan saddled Rocky, grabbed a rifle and a handful of ammunition. He had no idea what he was chasing other than his herd as he swung into his saddle and took off. At least the sky had started to clear, and off in the distance, he could see Five Paws.

Rocky barreled ahead as though he, too, were being chased. Duncan leaned forward and allowed Rocky to gallop at full speed. Ahead of Duncan was his herd, but he wasn't close enough to see what kept them running. Then he heard the bark. Wolves!

His gut tightened and anger flowed through him. Five Paws had veered off with the hopes of stopping the stampede. Duncan fired several shots through the night air, hoping to scare away the wolves, but they weren't going to give up. They were probably hungry, and the herd was food for the taking. Duncan gained on the herd just in time to see the wolves down a calf.

Damnation! That calf would have been a hefty profit this spring, and now it was food for the predators. He rode ahead, leaving the wolves to their meal, and continued the attempt to turn the herd. The sun was coming up by the time he and Five Paws had managed to slow the herd and bring it around to the east, far from the hungry beasts that had snatched a piece of Duncan's profit.

Every time Duncan attempted to count the heads, he came up with a different number. Leaving a lone animal behind would probably guarantee its death. He'd have to reride. For the time being, this pack would eat their fill, then he and Five Paws could chase the wolves back into the mountains, far away from his ranch.

He knew people who ate wolf meat, and probably Five Paws and Dora would have eaten it. But Duncan had no desire to eat a wolf. His anger kept him awake, but the gentle rock in the saddle lulled him in the cold morning air as he kept the herd moving towards home.

"I ride back." Five Paws turned his horse.

Duncan nodded. He was too tired to care what Five Paws did or if he shot a wolf.

Duncan tried counting again and this

time he was so short that he realized he could no longer think straight. With the cattle nearing the lower portion of the pasture, he wasn't certain he had the energy to put out food for them, but he knew that the corn would keep them where they belonged. He opened the barn door and discovered Zadie waiting for him.

"What happened?"

"Wolves."

"You look terrible. How much food do they get? I'll give it to them."

He shook his head and pushed past her.

She watched what he did, but any attempt to help seemed to put her in his path, and he wasn't happy. When he finished, he didn't stop to eat. He went straight to his room.

I'm doing it again. I'm failing to give her credit for trying.

Zadie had spent almost three hours pacing in the barn and wondering what was wrong. The cold had sunk into her bones. Her feet and fingertips were almost numb, and yet, she wanted to go after Duncan. She'd sensed danger and had known to stay away until it was over. Now he was back, and she still didn't know exactly what had happened other than there had been a wolf. There were wolves in Virginia, but they never came into town.

She followed him into the house, and when he wordlessly vanished behind his bedroom door, she went to her own. She'd only had four hours of sleep, for she'd had too much on her mind when she'd gone to bed. There was one thing she knew for certain; she didn't want to lose Duncan. Nor did she want to lose herself in a marriage.

There was no question about being attracted to him. He was a beautiful man - the kind of man that Michelangelo would paint or sculpt. Duncan was perfectly proportioned from what Zadie could tell, and she wouldn't have minded trying her hand at drawing a nude of him. That thought sent heat racing to her cheeks. She snuggled under her quilt in an attempt to warm her half-frozen body.

"Zadie, wake up. Are you ill?"

Zadie opened her eyes at the sound of Abilene's voice. "No, I'm fine. I was cold and sleepy. Have you talked to Duncan?"

"No."

"Is he awake?"

"He left here about an hour ago mumbling something about wolves." Abilene shook her head. "I haven't seen a man work as hard as him since I was a young girl."

Zadie knew wolves were dangerous

animals and were natural predators on a ranch, but she also saw them as magnificent creatures. Their fur was splendid. She discovered she had contradictory feelings about them. Duncan, do you feel that way too? Or am I alone with such thoughts?

She pulled herself from the bed and began to assess her situation. In spite of not having drapes at the windows, the house was still warm and there were no drafts around the glass. She walked down the hall to the bathing room. There she dropped the stopper into the sink and turned on the hot water tap. When the sink was half full of steaming water, she added some cold from the other tap. Then she washed for the day. This was a luxury she didn't have in Virginia, and she loved it.

Duncan hadn't just built a house for her; he added all sorts of lovely touches to it. Guilt crawled up her spine as she realized what she had failed to see. She had only looked at things from her side and not from his. But she still wasn't certain if she could unconditionally give him her heart. But she did know she had to thank him for what he had provided for her.

***

With Five Paws' help, Duncan counted his herd again. They were short three head. They needed to chase the wolves and look for the missing livestock. Bitter cold air blew, and from the looks of the gray sky, they should waste no time beginning their search.

They rode to where the calf had been downed and found the wolves sleeping nearby. Duncan nodded to Five Paws and they began their chase close to the remnants of the mostly eaten carcass. They rode hard and shot into the air, keeping the wolves moving. After chasing the pack across several small streams, they watched them cross to the other side of a river. That's when Duncan decided he'd had enough. He had no desire to get wet or to make Rocky swim in the icy cold water. He fired his gun several more times, watching the pack continue to run until they had vanished into a stand of distant scrub. Then Duncan turned around, and in the waning light of day, they headed home.

It was well after dark when he returned to the barn. He still had evening chores, and he was completely exhausted. But when he saw Dora Grace, he smiled, hoping one day Zadie's belly would hold his child. She took his horse and handed him a note from Zadie.

He took the paper and read it. The weight rolled off of him, but it left behind a feeling of remorse for not telling Zadie what he was doing. "Come, Five Paws. We have a meal waiting for us."

They washed at the sink in the barn before going to the house. The light shining through the window lit their path as flurries floated through the air. He wondered what he'd be facing tomorrow.

***

Zadie began to heat the meals for the men when she saw them ride up. Relief washed over her. She had spent the entire afternoon fretting over Duncan's wellbeing when he hadn't returned in a timely manner. As the men walked into the kitchen, she couldn't stop her bright smile, for she now knew they were safe. "I was so worried about you. Is everything all right?"

"We're down a few head. We'll go looking tomorrow morning. What do I smell?"

"Goose. You can thank Dora Grace. She killed it."

"I can't think of the last time I ate goose. How did she--"

Zadie giggled. "I never saw anyone do that, but she threw a knife at it."

Five Paws smiled and Duncan nodded. "It seems as though the Indians all know how to toss spears and throw knives. I think it starts as a childhood game."

"Abilene was happy. She did the actual cooking, and I made the dessert. Have some of Abilene's orange gravy with the goose. It is delicious. She made it with dried oranges."

"I have to go back outside. I still have evening chores."

"No, you don't. I did them."

Duncan plunked his elbows on the table and put his head into his hands. "Zadie, I don't know what to say. You shouldn't be doing my chores."

"You weren't here, and I knew they needed to be done. Dora Grace helped me. I told you, I don't worry about whose job something is, only that it is done. If I can help I will." She put the plates on the table.

He looked up at her with tired eyes, but he sat up straighter. "I need to tell you thank you for this hot meal, but also for your help. I've been amiss by not expressing my appreciation over your willingness to do things for me."

"Duncan, eat. I've been worried about you all day." She served him dessert. "I'm going to go upstairs and draw a warm bath for you. I'm certain it will help you feel better after your time in the saddle."

"I'm too tired."

"I promise you will sleep better after a bath. Leave the dishes and I'll get them later."

She ran up the stairs and to his room.

She found a union suit for him along with a pair of socks and put them in the bathing room. After filling the tub, she placed a towel and his union suit over the hot water pipe that went to the sink, knowing a warmed towel and a toasty union suit would soothe him, body and soul.

As she was finishing up, he appeared in the doorway. "Why do you do this for me?"

She gave him her best smile and left. "I'll check on you in a few minutes."

She walked down the back staircase to the kitchen. Why do you think, Duncan? She giggled to herself. Because I really do care about you, and you stink.

After cleaning up the kitchen, she glanced out the window and saw Five Paws and Dora Grace walking hand-in-hand to their cabin. Zadie admired the woman. Any woman in Franklin that Zadie had known usually took to her bed when in Dora Grace's condition. But Dora Grace never stopped. She acted as though it was nothing, even though her abdomen bulged.

Zadie realized they were a happy couple. It was obvious in the way they looked at each other and in the things that Dora Grace did for him. Five Paws would often give Dora Grace some tiny gift such as a flower blossom or some tiny stone that he picked up, and each gift was accepted with a smile as though it were a prized item.

Zadie washed the dishes and put them away. She checked everything carefully, snuffed the lights, except for a small lantern she carried, and went upstairs. The bathing room was dark, and she realized Duncan had drained the tub. But his clothes were in a pile against the wall. As she walked the hallway to her own room, she noticed he hadn't even bothered to close his bedroom door. The sounds of his slumber were evident. Stepping into his room, she put the tiny lantern on his chest of drawers and went to him. She leaned over and kissed his cheek. The sweet scent of soap lingered on him. "Please sleep tonight. You need it."

In her room, his question haunted her. Why had she done his chores? Was she not taking care of him as a woman cares for her husband? Why did she draw his bath? Why didn't she simply tell him to take one and allow him to fill the tub?

She sat by her window, as she had done hundreds of times in Franklin, and stared into the night. Questions swirled in her mind. One question dominated. Am I ready to become Duncan's wife?

12

Zadie woke to sunshine, but her room was cold. She pulled the blanket tighter to her body, wishing she had worn heavy woolen stockings. After shivering for several more minutes, she decided to go to the bathing room where it was always toasty warm.

It was only slightly warmer in there, but it was enough to dress for the day. When she went downstairs, the house was quiet...abandoned, and the kitchen stove was barely warm. After adding several pieces of wood to the stove, she realized the coffee was cold and began to reheat what was left in the pot. Where is everyone?

It didn't look as though anyone had fixed breakfast. Maybe they washed and put everything away. Confused, she sat at the kitchen table while she thought about it. She heard the clock in the hallway strike eleven and knew she had overslept. Another group of questions formed in her mind, for she had not slept that late since she was a young girl. She decided that the last few weeks had been emotionally difficult, and the travel here had only made it worse. Now that she was here, life was fraught with tribulations. She could almost hear her father saying 'sleep heals the body and the soul'. I need to heal.

Duncan came in looking for dinner and she hadn't made anything.

"Oh, I'm glad to see you. Where is everyone?"

"At the cabin helping Dora Grace. Did you just wake up?"

She nodded. "There were leftovers from last night, or would you prefer bacon and eggs?"

"We are out of eggs. I need to go to town. Would you like to come?" Duncan smiled.

"Yes. There's quite a long list of things that we need. I'm certain Abilene would like to go, too."

Duncan shook his head. "Not today."

Duncan made a circle with his arms and hands in front of his belly. "Her time has come."

"Dora Grace? Today?" She grinned. "That's why everyone's at the cabin?"

Duncan nodded.

"Oh, how exciting."

Abilene often acted as a midwife for those who couldn't afford Dr. Larkford's services or didn't want a man present. Dora Grace was in good hands. But now Zadie was torn between being with Duncan and being with Dora Grace.

Zadie toasted three rolls in the oven and filled them with leftover goose meat. She gave two rolls to Duncan and then she ate one. She could barely contain her excitement. "I don't want to leave the ranch and Dora Grace, but I can't wait to go into town for supplies. I hate making these types of decisions."

"I'll make it for you. Dora Grace has help, but we're out of supplies. Come with me."

Zadie nodded.

Duncan looked at her and grinned. "You were right. The bath did wonders. Ever notice when you're exhausted that sleep doesn't always come easily?"

"Yes."

"Ever feel as though your body trembles as it tries to relax?"

She nodded. "I hate that feeling. That's

overworked muscles trying to readjust."

"It didn't happen to me. I could barely pull myself from the tub. But I had a wonderful warm towel and a warm Union suit to wear. I merely stumbled my way to my bed. I think I was asleep before my head was on the pillow."

"I'm glad. I could tell you were tired by the dark circles under your eyes."

"It's not easy living on a ranch."

***

Duncan hitched Nellie to the buckboard and brought it to the house. "Ready?"

"Yes. And I have a long list of things I want to buy."

"Zadie, I only have a small amount of money."

"Ah, yes. But my mother has money to pay her way. I will pay for much of it. Consider it rent."

Duncan shook his head.

But Zadie handed him several dollars.

"This is enough for several months of food."

"No, it's not. We need supplies. This is going to be an expensive trip. Stay with me in town and I will show you. First, we will buy what we absolutely must have. If there is money left, you may spend it on whatever you want."

Once in town, he took Zadie into the mercantile for the dry goods she needed.

"Buy what we must have." He watched what she bought, and he was glad she'd offered him money. She bought clothes pins and yarn. A dozen spices, and a large quantity of flour along with other kitchen supplies. He was certain she would buy the entire store, but he didn't say a word.

He paid for everything and then loaded everything into the buckboard while she went into the butcher's shop. Did he dare to go to the bakery and see if they had his favorite? They cost a few cents, but with all the extra mouths to feed... The delicious, sticky treats, all wrapped with cinnamon and raisins, tugged at him. After some quick pondering, he went into the shop and looked in the glass-fronted cabinet that contained a variety of desserts. They only had four of those rolls left.

There was another woman buying several things, and when she went to the display case, he held his breath as she pointed to two items. Please don't take those rolls. A man wanted two loaves of bread. Duncan could only stand and await his turn.

"I'd like to buy those." He pointed to the buns. He paid the two cents and took the paper wrapped rolls. Then the little nagging doubt began to poke at him. Will she be upset if I tell her how much I like these? Will she think I don't like her cooking? All the negative questions ran through his mind and each one stabbed at him. I'll tell her I love them and maybe she can figure out how to make them. Please don't hate me, Zadie, for liking another woman's baking.

Zadie walked out of the butcher's shop with her arms full, and he immediately went to her. "Oh, I'm so sorry." He took her packages. "I didn't mean to leave you for so long." He loaded the meats into the buckboard. "Give me a moment to pay for all of this."

"Don't bother. I did. It was only four dollars and eighteen cents."

"Don't use the word only when saying four dollars. That's expensive. And we have plenty of deer meat. What did you buy?"

She placed her hand on his arm. "Food for all of us. Don't worry about it. What if it snows, and we can't get here for two or three weeks? You said the weather can be horrid. Now we are prepared."

"I wish you had let me pay for it. A gentleman doesn't have his woman paying for things. He pays for them."

Zadie rolled her eyes at him. "That's ridiculous. Abilene paid for things all the time. My father gave her money and she used it. It was nothing for me to do the same. No one knows whose money it is. If they think it's mine, then they will think I'm a lucky woman to not have to rely on my husband. If they think it is yours, then they will think that you trust me."

"I see your point."

"And what did you buy?"

He swallowed the hard lump that had instantly formed. "My favorite buns. They are rolled, and they are sticky and delicious."

She unfolded a corner of the paper wrapping and peered at them. "I've tasted them. You've brought them home."

He looked towards the farm supply and decided there had been enough money spent. Then he turned back to her and grinned. "I'm hoping you can figure out how to make them."

"Oh, we're both going to hope that Abilene can do that. She's much more skilled than I am."

He gave her what he hoped was his best smile. That will save a few pennies, and with luck, they will be available more often. "Then I will look forward to tasting her recipe." He helped Zadie onto the buckboard. "We only need to stop at the post office, and then we can go home."

"Duncan, you said there's a church in town. I'd like to go there before we leave."

"I don't know if the preacher is in town."

"Please, may we check?"

"Yes." I'll never understand you, Zadie.

Are you looking to go to church or are you finally considering marriage?

***

Zadie held tightly to the bench as Duncan pulled the buckboard to the side of the church. Attached to the side of the building was a small residence.

Duncan set the brake. "With the smoke coming from the chimney, I'd say someone is there."

Zadie smiled at him. "I'll only be a minute."

She scampered off the buckboard and down the path before Duncan could say more to her. Her skin tingled with anticipation as she knocked on the door of the residence and waited.

And elderly man answered. "Good afternoon. How may I help you?"

She glanced over her shoulder and then turned back to the slightly balding, white-haired man. "Are you the preacher?"

"Yes, I am. Please come in. It's too cold to hold the door open."

"Thank you, Pastor." Zadie stepped into a tiny parlor that was the size of what Duncan had at the cabin. The kitchen was straight ahead, and off to the side, a colorful quilt at the foot of a bed peeked through a partially opened door. "I came to inquire about marriage."

"Did you want to be married today?"

"Oh, no. I was thinking that... maybe... Christmas Eve might be a good day."

The man furrowed his brow, went to his desk, and opened a book. "What time?"

"Could we do it in the afternoon?"

"I can do it at four p.m. I'll be gone in the morning but I should be home by two."

"That would work. Of course, if the

weather--"

"Yes, the weather can be a problem. I'll understand. Now I need your name and the name of the lucky man."

"Zadie Larkford and Duncan Lorde, with an e on the end of Lorde."

"Oh, yes. He's a fine fellow. Doesn't get to church much, but it's difficult for the ranchers to come to town."

Zadie nodded. "Thank you, Pastor. Weather permitting, we will be here Christmas Eve."

She asked a few more questions about weekly services before thanking the man one more time. Then with a light step, she returned to Duncan.

"What was that about?" Duncan helped her onto her seat.

"I was checking on services. We always went to church back home, especially on Christmas."

Duncan nodded, and Zadie knew he wasn't thrilled. That would be two days a week that he'd be coming into town. But her mother always went and expected Zadie to go.

She could feel her heart beating as though it were a butterfly flapping its wings. She would have liked a special dress for her wedding, but she had the dress that Ethel made last year for Christmas. It was lovely and Zadie knew it would be perfect for the occasion.

She wondered if Duncan would shave his beard for the wedding. But asking him to do that was asking to remove the protective covering to his face as he worked in the bitter cold. He looks so much better without it.

As soon as they returned home, Zadie went to the cabin. Dora Grace had given birth to a little boy.

Abilene beamed with pride. "He slipped

out without any problems. That baby was anxious to meet his mother and father."

"So Dora Grace is doing well?"

"She's wonderful, but she keeps trying to do things. She doesn't seem to understand that she must stay quiet."

"Is she sleeping?"

"No. Five Paws is with her. He's strutting around like any proud poppa."

Zadie giggled. She knew the man loved his wife and was anxious for a son. Sons were valuable and daughters were not. Zadie was lucky that her poppa was content with a daughter. She went to the door and rapped lightly. "May I see the baby?"

Five Paws opened the door.

Dora Grace had the baby tucked in her arms but offered the infant to Zadie.

"Oh, he's beautiful!" He was swaddled in rabbit fur. Zadie ran her fingertips over the dark locks on the baby's head. She rubbed his cheek and he instantly turned towards her touch. "I have nothing for you, baby boy." She gazed at his parents. "What is his name?"

Five Paws said, "Wanji."

Zadie knew that was their word for one. Zadie smiled. "Wanji. Yes, he is your first. But you know he will need an English name that we will file with the Bureau of Indian Affairs. May we call him Benji, which is short for Benjamin? It is a fine English name."

Five Paws and Dora Grace exchanged a few words. From Dora Grace's bright smile, Zadie knew she had found the perfect name for the little boy.

Five Paws nodded. "Benjamin."

She smiled at the sleeping baby in her arms. Dark fuzz covered his head and his eyelashes were little dark fringes on his cheeks. Her heart melted.

With that, the baby began to fuss, and Zadie returned the infant to his mother. The wonderful feeling that came while holding the newborn filled Zadie, and she wondered what it would be like to hold her own child. She wasn't Catherine. Zadie never was one for playing with dolls, but since meeting Duncan everything had changed. Can I, too, someday be a mother? Do I really want to be a mother?

As she walked back to her house, she thought about Catherine's boisterous little ones and then remembered the grandparents who didn't want the children's presence. Benji was a welcomed child on the ranch, and he would have plenty of room to run and play. If Duncan and I have children, they will be loved not only by us, but by my mother and Abilene. Is that not why Abilene insisted on coming?

The image of a reading a bedtime story to her child floated through her mind, as did the image of her teaching that child to read and draw. Maybe having a child means giving up some things, but maybe it also means I become more. Will Duncan be more than a man who appears for meals and expects his children to be perfectly groomed angels?

***

Duncan smiled when the sun shone brightly and melted the snow. It was an answer to his prayer. For four days, he and Five Paws moved cattle so they were by the hayricks. That's when he discovered he had not lost a single head, other than that calf, to the wolves. He had actually gained three. With no idea whose brand was on them, he'd have to ask when he went to town.

But a few nights later, the wind howled as he went to bed. Wind meant foul weather, and he wasn't thrilled, but he was glad they had moved the cattle. That would take some stress off of him. He closed his eyes to the night sounds and then woke abruptly to the sound of a crash.

He listened, trying to discern what he had heard. Then he heard a metallic squeal. He ran down the stairs and looked out the kitchen window. It took a second to comprehend what he was seeing. His windmill was on the ground. Five Paws was walking towards the downed metal as Duncan opened the back door. "Come in and wait. You can't fix it alone."

Duncan was glad he'd been in the habit of preparing the coffee for morning before retiring. Without a windmill, there would be no water, because that's what pumped the water from the ground to the house, barn, and cabin. He started the coffee and then went upstairs. In his room, he dressed in his warmest clothes. In his mind, he reviewed several possible ways to return the heavy thing to an upright position. Then he'd still have pipes to fix. The uncertainty of having running water any time soon, no matter how he looked at the situation, weighed on him.

"It's not going anywhere." Duncan began to fix breakfast.

"We not fix alone. We need more hands."

"I know, but we don't have any. We have to manage with the two of us."

"No. Need more hands."

They ate their breakfast and faced the difficult chore in the bitter cold wind. Duncan removed the twisted sails from the windmill and placed them inside the barn. Then they started on the frame. No matter how hard they tried, they couldn't get it to stand upright. It only wanted to slide along the ground.

The sky was no longer pitch dark and they hadn't managed to accomplish much. Duncan knew he was in trouble. Pulling the heavy thing upright was only part of the battle, it would have to be anchored into the ground. Considering it had been ripped from its foundation, they would have to improvise.

"You're right. We can't do it."

"You need it held here. Then we pull. Need more hands."

"All I have is Zadie."

"She help."

"No. She's a woman. I can't ask her to do a man's job. It's not a simple clothesline. This is hard work."

They tried several more times and finally gave up. The cold penetrated every part of Duncan's body until he was certain he could no longer use his hands. It was all he could do to open the back door to his house. Once inside, he stood by the stove. Five Paws is right. I need to ask Zadie to help.

Sufficiently thawed enough to even think about climbing the stairs, he went to Zadie. He stood outside her door and hesitated. He didn't want to wake her mom or Abilene. There was nothing they could do. After a moment, he decided to merely open Zadie's door and go to her.

Her long dark braid rested partially across her pillow and partially on her quilt. He picked up the end of the silky tress. I can't ask her. It's too much.

She rolled over and her hands went to her eyes, which fluttered as she awakened. "Duncan?"

He dropped her braid. "Zadie. I know I shouldn't ask. It's not right to ask a woman to do a man's job. Will you please help me?"

"Huh?" Her fingertips rubbed her eyes.

She sat up and pulled her quilt tight to her body. "What's wrong?"

"The windmill. It's fallen. I need another set of hands."

She pulled the covers back and began to stand. Her flannel nightgown showed off her pert figure. The feeling that flowed through him was not what he needed under the circumstances. She slipped into her robe and pulled it closed.

"Remember there is no water. It's the windmill that supplies our water. It's bitter cold out there. I'll grab a union suit for you. You'll need it."

"Thank you."

"One more thing. Wear the warmest you have and be prepared to work from Rocky."

***

Duncan left, leaving Zadie feeling perplexed. No water. She tiptoed to the bathing room and then back to her room where she found Duncan's union suit lying on her bed. She pulled it on and she swam in it, but it would be warmer than her chemise. She already knew what cold was like and from what he said, she knew it was going to be brutal. Sitting on her bed, she managed to pull on a pair of silk stockings with a wool pair over them and a pair of wool socks on top. Then she pulled on a riding skirt, and a heavy twill skirt over that, except she couldn't manage to get the last button closed on it. She couldn't even find a belt to work with it. I'll borrow one from Duncan.

With her feet jammed into boots, she went to the kitchen, holding his belt. She smiled and held the old belt out to him. "It's too big. Will you put an extra hole in it for me?"

"There's no need for that." He took the belt from her, frowned, and tied a knot in the leather belt. "Now try."

"I can't get the knot through the loops."

He untied it. "Put it on until you reach the back. I'll knot it on you."

She nodded and did as she was told. Five Paws handed her a cup of coffee and a toasted roll with jam. "I thought you said there was no water."

"Only what was placed in the pot before we all retired. And there's no snow to scoop."

"But there's plenty of ice in the cold cellar. We should bring a block in."

Five Paws stepped out the back door and Zadie smiled as she found a large pan to hold the melting water. She put the pan in the sink, and when Five Paws entered holding a block, she pointed and watched as he placed the block on its end inside the pan. She left a note on the table and then followed the men outside.

She could feel the hairs in her nose freezing as she wrapped one of Duncan's bandanas around her face and then covered it with her scarf. Wearing delicate dress gloves with wool over them, she pulled her heavy leather gloves over the other pairs. Still the cold seeped to her bones.

She followed Duncan into the barn wondering what she would be doing. It was cold in the barn, but at least, the wind wasn't blowing.

"I'll saddle Rocky. I need you to keep him tugging on the rope, while we pull in the opposite direction."

As soon as Rocky's girth was cinched, she hoisted herself into his saddle and patted his neck. "Looks as though we're in for a long morning, baby boy. Are you ready?"

Duncan led her to the spot where he wanted her to start, and then walked away.

Rocky pranced in the cold weather and she hunkered over the horse in an attempt to stay out of the wind. A minute later, Duncan returned and tied a rope to Rocky's saddle horn.

"All you are going to do is to hold this rope steady. With Nellie's help, we will do all the pulling. And when I say to stop, you stop! I don't want to send the windmill onto the barn or onto us. Do you understand?"

"Yes. You pull and I hold." She looked behind her. Nellie was tied to a rope that ran through a pulley attached to the barn. There was a third rope that Five Paws was handling.

As Duncan walked away, he hollered, "Remember, this is for your water and your convenience."

She laughed and hollered back to him, "Wrong, Mr. Lorde! I believe this is your windmill and your ranch."

She heard him yell to Five Paws to start

pulling. She watched as her rope tightened and she tried to hold Rocky steady. The men attempted several times to right the fallen windmill. Each time she watched them and she thought about her science classes. She had hated science. It was a subject that she had to complete to graduate. Her father hadn't been able to understand her dislike of what he'd considered a fascinating field. That's why you became a doctor, Poppa, and I'm an artist.

But there was something wrong. She knew it. She stared into the night at his ropes and how the one went to the large pulley over the door to the barn's loft. Then she remembered studying pulleys and fulcrums. Like a bolt of lightning, it hit her. As they were getting ready to attempt another pull, she called, "Duncan! I want to talk to you."

He came to her. "What? I'm busy, in case you haven't noticed."

She told him what she thought he should be doing, and he stared at her.

"Please, Duncan. I had to study this in college and I never dreamed I'd need this knowledge. A man can push a boxcar filled with coal on the rails if it's in motion, but if it is not, he can push against it forever and it won't move. You're trying to move that boxcar."

She told him how to re-sling the ropes, and he still continued to stare at her as though she were daft.

"We're trying to move a windmill, not a train."

"I know that. But it all has to do with weight. Oh, please, try it my way. If it doesn't work, you can go back to tugging on this thing for the next four hours."

He started to walk away.

"I can't feel my toes. If there's not some sort of progress, I'm going back to the house and climbing under my warm quilt until I thaw."

She watched him walk to Five Paws, but she couldn't hear what he was saying. She wasn't joking about leaving him for her warm blankets - she was freezing.

A moment later, he retied all the ropes.

"Tie that one higher!" she yelled. "As close to the top as you can." Then she waited.

It took several minutes before they were ready to try again. But when Duncan hollered to pull, this time the windmill lifted until the rope snapped and the windmill fell to the ground. She waited while Duncan found a new piece of rope and tied it. When the signal came to pull, the windmill lifted off the ground and came to a standing position.

Duncan cheered and hurried to stabilize the tall structure with ropes.

Five Paws climbed the structure with the agility of a cat and tied several ropes that were then tethered to the ground and the barn.

Duncan ran back to her and took the rope that had been tied to Rocky. "I love you, Zadie Larkford!

Knowing it would be hours before they'd have it secured and then several more hours before it would be operational, she unhooked Rocky and returned him to the barn. She rewarded Rocky with a handful of wheat berries mixed with a little corn. Then she removed his saddle. Dawn still had not broken as she made her way to the house. Abilene was already in the kitchen.

"I'm certain the men will be hungry. And I can't feel my fingers or toes. I'm going to bed."

Abilene shook her head. "That was a man's job. He had no right to ask you."

Zadie laughed. "It least he asked. I didn't mind helping. In fact, it felt good to know that I could assist. I get the impression that a ranch is a joint effort."

Duncan almost couldn't believe what had happened. Looking at her configuration for the ropes made perfect sense. Why didn't I see it? But he didn't have time to ponder his situation, getting the structure secured was of the utmost importance. An hour later, he went into his house where Abilene fed him hot coffee and a large bowl of grits with cheese. He couldn't remember the last time he'd eaten grits, and their warm natural sweetness slid down his throat like manna. Even Five Paws smiled as he ate his.

When Duncan finished his breakfast of eggs, grits, and bacon, he said, "Thank you, Abilene. That was the best breakfast I've had since I left Edenton."

"Grits are a poor man's breakfast, but I think they stick to the ribs. And you men need something to stick tight after what you've been doing."

He could barely keep his eyes open, and he knew he had more to do. But before he closed them, he needed to apologize to Zadie. He rapped lightly on her door and entered.

She didn't stir.

He approached her bed, and then kissed her cheek. "I love you, Zadie. You are everything I ever wanted and more."

Her eyes fluttered open.

"You were right, thank you. It was your knowledge that saved us. I only wish you had figured out what we were doing wrong sooner."

"I hated science. But there was this little drawing on a page. I remembered the drawing."

"Forgive me for not letting you into my life completely. I've failed to recognize your ability and your willingness to help. I've acted like a fool. I never dreamed a woman could be as capable as you."

He kissed her lips and she wrapped her arms around his neck, pulling him off balance and onto her bed. Their kiss deepened and he was lost in it.

***

Zadie realized he'd fallen asleep kissing her. She tossed her side of the quilt over his body as she slipped from under him. Good night or good morning, I'm not sure which to wish you.

With Duncan's arm draped over her, she drifted into a deep slumber only to be awakened by Abilene. "Are you going to sleep all day?"

Zadie touched her finger to her lips.

"No. He's got work to do. You may sleep tonight. You are in trouble with your mother. Deal with it. You're no longer a child."

13

Zadie pulled herself from her bed, gathered her clothes for the day, and scurried to the bathing room where Abilene had left a pan of simmering water on the small bathroom stove. Zadie ladled some into a bowl. Using a cloth, she washed her face and then put on fresh clothes.

She had faced her father over many infractions, but having a man in her bedroom was considered unthinkable. Having him in her bed was even worse. A knot began to form in her insides. She couldn't really remember her mother ever being angry with her.

She peered into the large mirror and tried to tell herself that all would be well. It was as though she already knew what her mother would say. The knot that had begun to form untangled, and she found herself giggling.

She had no reason to hide from Duncan. Marriage was merely a formality, for she had never felt as close to anyone as she had to him. Hadn't she been waiting for Duncan to see her as more than a woman who would wash his clothes and cook for him? Oh, and that kiss. She tingled at the thought. I want those kisses everyday.

When she walked past her room, it was empty and so was Duncan's. She hoped to find him in the kitchen. Instead her mother was waiting for her, along with a bowl of grits.

"Good morning or is it afternoon?" She smiled at her mother as she lifted the bowl from the stove and added a dollop of butter to it.

Her mother frowned. "Did we send you to college to become a loose woman?"

Her mother's tirade continued, and Zadie waited for her mother to say it. Here it comes.

"If your father were alive--"

She couldn't stop the bubbling that rolled out as laughter. She reined it in and answered, "If my father were alive, he'd be thrilled to see that Duncan and I are doing so well. Don't forget, this was his idea. He wanted us together. And although it may not have looked very good, we were both dressed in layers of clothing because we had spent most of the night in this horrible cold weather trying to restore water to this ranch."

She sat at the kitchen table, scooped a spoonful of grits and put them in her mouth. I'm too old for my mother's disapproval.

"You're not married to him!"

With her spoon poised halfway between her bowl and her mouth, she raised her eyebrows and stared at her mother. "Momma, what difference does a few days make? The only thing he did was kiss me, and I promise it was the most wonderful kiss until he fell asleep doing it."

"He fell asleep kissing you? How dare he! And what's this about a few days? What are you saying?"

Zadie laughed so hard she didn't dare take another bite of food. "I told Duncan I'd marry him when I was ready. I haven't told him, so please keep my secret, but I'm hoping to be married on Christmas Eve. Oh, Momma, you and Poppa were right. He is a wonderful man who I know will take care of me. And he treats me well."

"Marriage?"

"Yes, Momma. I think I knew it from the

first few letters we exchanged. He was so funny, and kind - no matter what I wrote to him."

"What did you write? Did it match that horrible picture you sent that looked a tad bit like Mrs. Finnegan? You should have never sent that picture."

"Oh, that was a joke. His father already told him I was pretty. You never saw the horrible thing he sent me that he drew of him and Rocky. I promise Rocky was by far the better looking of the two."

"So you have finally consented to be his wife?"

"I haven't told him. Please allow me to do that when I am ready."

"But if you intend to marry him on Christmas Eve, that doesn't give us much time. There's not enough time to have a dress made for you. What will you wear?"

"Momma, do not fret. It will be a simple

wedding. I'll wear my dress from last Christmas."

"Christmas is not that far away, but having Duncan in your bedroom and in your bed--"

"Momma, he fell asleep. He knows I am not a whore or lacking morals. Duncan is very much a gentleman." She giggled. "Except when he is teasing."

Zadie's mother gave her daughter what Zadie thought of as the evil glare, but she knew her mother had fallen in love with Duncan and would be proud to have him as a son-in-law.

"We must make plans. My daughter must have a proper wedding."

Zadie finished her bowl of grits. She grinned as she took her bowl to the sink, knowing the distraction of a wedding would make her mother forget the incident with Duncan. "I wonder if we will need another block of ice or if he'll have the water restored later today."

Abilene was spending part of her day with Dora Grace who acted as though having a baby was as normal as having a cup of coffee, and Abilene kept fussing that Dora Grace was doing too much. Wanting to hold the newborn, Zadie joined them.

Abilene insisted that Dora Grace rest while the baby slept.

"I cook. I wash," Dora Grace protested.

Zadie giggled. "Oh, Dora Grace, let Abilene help. She loves babies."

"Yes. Baby sleep."

"Then let Abilene pamper you."

"Pammm?"

"Spoil."

"I no rot."

That sent Zadie into giggles. "Yes, make you so rotten that your are useless."

"You fun me?"

"Yes. She will care for you until you are like a child who no longer can do things for herself."

Dora Grace frowned and Zadie giggled. But as soon as the baby awakened, Zadie removed the wet diaper and tied a fresh one on him. Diapers were new to Dora Grace, who had only seen rabbit pelts as diapers, but she was adjusting very quickly to the white man's ways, and she embraced each new thing that she was taught. As Zadie turned to take the baby into the main room, Dora Grace was standing behind her.

Zadie smiled at her friend and then at the baby that she held in her arms. "He is a pretty baby. He looks like his poppa."

Dora Grace smiled brightly. "He has pretty name, too. Yes?"

"Yes."

Zadie laughed. "He's a royal little prince

around here with a very demanding cry. You'd think he was king...um, the chief of the household."

Zadie giggled as she passed the baby to his mother to be fed.

"All babies are demanding." Abilene huffed as she handed Dora Grace a cup of tea. "Drink."

Zadie turned to Dora Grace who had already begun nursing the infant. "I think Benjamin will grow up to be a fine young man like Benjamin Franklin."

Dora Grace pursed her lips and Zadie knew the new mother did not understand.

"Benjamin Franklin was an important man who did many wonderful things."

"Important. Yes. Baby important. Benjamin means important?"

"Benjamin is a name."

"He is a White man's chief?"

Zadie wrinkled her nose. How do I explain this? "No, Benjamin Franklin lived many years ago. He was not a chief, but he was a wise man to many chiefs."

"That is good name." Dora Grace nodded. "Dora Grace is pretty name. Duncan give it to me. He said I need pretty name."

"Yes. Dora Grace is pretty. Benjamin has a momma who is pretty with pretty name."

Dora Grace smiled and Zadie knew the young woman was happy.

***

Duncan came in exhausted. Every part of his body ached. The only thing that he had managed to do was to stabilize the windmill. But as he ate his supper, he realized the women were talking about some sort of party.

Zadie looked around the table and

announced her intention of going to bed early. "I've not had enough sleep."

"I second that." Duncan smiled. "I can barely keep my eyes open to eat, except I'm starving."

Abilene touched his arm. "How close are we to having water in the house?"

Duncan swallowed. "With luck, I will have the water restored and flowing sometime tomorrow. That is a vicious wind."

Abilene smiled. "This is a wonderful house. I've never seen one that lacked drafts the way this one does. You've done a fine job building it."

"Thank you." He turned to Zadie. "I'd like to speak with you for a moment before going to bed."

She nodded. "Yes. And I with you."

It was all Duncan could do to climb the stairs to the second floor, but Zadie followed him. When they reached the landing, he gently grasped her arm. "Thank you for all your help. I mean that. I was so tired and cold that I wasn't thinking clearly. Then you started talking about trains…"

"I'm sorry. It was all part of the same class."

"Then suddenly it clicked and I understood. I knew exactly what you were saying. It was leverage with a pulley."

She leaned against her doorframe and smiled at him. "I want to be your partner."

"You are more than…" He scuffed the heel of his boot against the wooden floor. "More than I ever dreamed I would find in a woman." He looked into her dark eyes. "I knew I wanted a wife. I asked my father for one, and I expected a complacent female who would be happy to be my bride. Instead, it seems I've found a wonderful friend."

She softly giggled. "When my father told

me he had arranged a marriage for me, I was livid. But by the time you had written that second letter to me, I knew you were special. Then I sent you that picture, and you sent your father..."

"I knew you were joking. It was your comment about Rocky. But it is more than that." He watched as Abilene came up the stairs and retired to her room. The older woman had also inched her way into his heart. "Life here isn't easy, but we're building something."

"You're not doing it alone. You are building a future for yourself, but also for Five Paws and his wife."

"I'm trying."

"I know we don't have water yet, but we will." She looked towards the ceiling. "My father was a man of his word." She dropped her gaze to Duncan. "He believed in people, and he understood that they are fallible. He also expected them to try to do their best. I can see that in you." She grinned. "I worry that I will not meet your expectations or manage to be what you think a wife should be. But I will try."

"Zadie..." He came to her and kissed her. "I never really thought I'd find love. I'm not certain what I thought a wife would be." He grinned. "A woman who could fix meals and... warm my bed."

She raised her eyebrows.

"Then my betrothed, who worried about tea parties and fox hunts, sent me her picture."

She pursed her lips. "I'm not beautiful, more on the tall and skinny side, but I doubt that I'm anything like that portrait I drew."

"No. You're beautiful, and your beauty goes far beyond the way you look." He swallowed. "Zadie, will you join me in my room tonight, because sleeping next to you was wonderful."

She shook her head. "Duncan, I can't. It's really not proper. You know that."

"I'm too tired to do more than sleep."

"Can you manage to wait until Christmas Eve?"

Laughter chuckled its way from someplace deep within him. "And what will be different about that night from this one, other then with luck, I won't be as tired?"

Her smile looked more like a smirk. "Kiss me, and then I'll tell you."

"Maybe you should tell me first. I fell asleep kissing you last time."

"Don't you dare fall asleep while standing on your feet."

He wrapped his arms around her and kissed her. It was warm and wonderful. Her slender body meshed with his. But he could feel the drain of his energy and the overwhelming need for sleep.

Breaking from the kiss, he stood back. "I can't keep going. I've got to sleep."

She grabbed his hand. "Remember when I said I'd let you know when I was ready to marry you."

He could feel his eyes closing and no longer had the stamina for more conversation. "Zadie, bed."

He turned away, but as he stepped over the threshold of his bedroom door, he could have sworn she said I'll marry you on Christmas Eve. None of it registered until he awakened with the oddest sensation that she had told him she'd marry him. Where did I get that? Did I dream it?

He pulled on his clothes as he tried to remember. She had told him before that she would marry him, but only when she was ready. The thought wouldn't go away. Of course, she'll marry me. She's promised me that much. That's why she's here. Did I walk away from her last night in the middle of an important conversation? What have I done?

Abilene was in the kitchen fixing breakfast. He poured a cup of coffee and waited. Breakfast was delicious. He never figured out how she managed to have everything ready at once, but she did. He had biscuits with sausage gravy, fried potatoes, and three eggs. And when he cleaned his plate, she placed a slice of hot apple pie in front of him. "What did I do to deserve dessert for breakfast?"

"Nothing. But you didn't stop yesterday for your dinner and I don't want you getting hungry."

She poured a cup of coffee and sat at the table with him. Abilene was different. His mother had hired help, but they never acted like family. Abilene did. Not that he minded. The old woman was easy to like, especially when she made him so many wonderful meals. But it was more than that. She mothered everyone, and from what Five Paws said, she was even doing it to Dora Grace.

"Now, you go out there this morning, and do what you need to do. Running water is much nicer than working with blocks of ice. Not that I can't make do, but you don't want to use up your ice. You have no idea what this summer will be like." She took another sip of coffee. "Besides by then, that pretty wife of yours will be with child. Mark my words."

"I can't think that far ahead. Not with what I'm facing out there." He jerked his hand in the direction of the windmill.

Abilene made a little sound, and he wasn't certain if she was showing her disapproval.

The old woman smiled. "She's like her poppa. She doesn't just look like him - she has his personality."

"I don't remember Mr. Larkford. I know he came to visit my father a few times, but that is all."

Abilene sipped at her coffee. "Her momma wasn't happy when she was with child. She was sick the whole time, and after Zadie came, she stayed in bed for months. Now if you ask me, that's not right. My grandmother had her babies in the tobacco fields and kept on working. Seems Dora Grace is of the same ilk, but I told her to enjoy a little pampering. Babies can be a lot of work, and as long as I'm here, I will help her." She shook her head. "I don't think she knows what I'm saying."

"She understands most words." He finished the coffee in his cup and then stood. "Excuse me, ma'am, but I have work to do." He pulled on his coat. "That was a delicious breakfast. Thank you."

"You go fix that water and stop wasting time."

"I will." He walked out the door. Five Paws was coming in from the field. "How are the cattle?"

"They good. We start on pipe?"

***

Zadie awakened late. Outside her bedroom window was a clear sky with only a few puffs of white clouds. She thought back to Duncan's lack of reaction to her announcement. She realized how tired he was and understood.

By now, she knew that the clear sky meant it would be cold. Dressed warmly, she was determined she would help Duncan. He's exhausted. If there is something I can do to lessen his burden, I will.

There was nothing that she knew about

pipes, but she was open to learning and doing what she could. She kept those thoughts in her mind as she went downstairs. "Good morning, Momma and Abilene. Something smells delicious."

Abilene went to the stove. "It's the sausage gravy you smell. I ran out of casings and I need to use up what is left."

"I could smell it as I came downstairs."

"I promise, Duncan ate a fair amount this morning. You would have thought he hadn't eaten in days. He's still a growing boy in my opinion."

Zadie's mother patted Abilene's arm. "He's not a boy. You used to say that about Gregory, and he was in his thirties, worrying about a few gray hairs he'd found."

Abilene laughed. "His poppa didn't go gray until the war came, and that was enough to make anyone's hair turn gray. And Gregory's grandpoppa barely had any gray when he died." Abilene served a biscuit loaded in sausage and gravy to Zadie. "Are you going to eat more?"

"This is plenty. Thank you."

Zadie's mom excused herself. "I must prepare for the day and my daughter's upcoming wedding."

Zadie nodded.

Abilene sat at the table. "Everyone knew the war was coming." She had a wistful look on her face. "Your grandmomma was afraid to stay on the plantation. She wanted to go to her parents' in Richmond where it would be safer. She said that Richmond would be defended, no matter what. So Albert took her there. Gregory was in medical school in Pennsylvania and Simon was working on the plantation. Your grandpoppa, Albert, wanted Simon to go to school, too, but he was sweet on a girl and didn't want to leave with Gregory. Simon had gone off one night with his girl, and I was in the house with Albert."

Abilene picked up her cup of coffee and took a sip. "All the others were hunkered down in their quarters for the evening. Simon came back and told us there was troop movement nearby. Albert ordered everyone to douse all fires and to remain quiet. I cannot remember a night I was ever more afraid." Abilene smiled. "But Albert stayed with me."

"You loved him, didn't you?"

The woman reached over and patted Zadie's hand. "With all my heart."

Do I dare ask? "Is Simon my uncle?"

Abilene stood and began to collect dishes. "Now, don't you worry your pretty little head about a bunch of fools. The war is over, and your poppa came home. That's all that matters."

"My father knew, didn't he?"

"It was a long time ago. You have that wonderful man out there and you need to help plan this wedding. Your momma wants an announcement made. She said if we do the wedding in town at the church, then we need a reception afterwards. Being it will be Christmas the next day, we're planning on Christmas as being the start of the receiving of guests. But I'm going to do a cake with an icing of butter, cream, and sugar that we can take to the church with us." Abilene lifted Zadie's empty plate. "I need to take care of these."

"I'll create some announcements. Are you certain that you don't want help with this morning's dishes?"

Abilene shooed Zadie away.

In her room, Zadie removed several sheets of paper from her letterbox and began to make some invitations. One for each

Barrett store, one for the church, one for the post office, the bakery, and one for the butcher.

She laid them out, letting the ink dry before she began to decorate each one with pretty bows and ribbons using her Conté sticks. She didn't realize that her morning had slipped away until her momma knocked on the bedroom door.

"Momma, come see what I have made. They must be delivered to town."

"Oh, they are perfect. Your poppa would love to be here and see this. In fact, I think he would like it here. He was used to the country, having grown up outside of Courtland, Virginia." She walked to a window. "It's beautiful out there. And where is the dress that you intend to use for your wedding?"

Zadie went to a chest and withdrew her Christmas dress. "Here. It's clean and only needs pressing."

"Yes, that is lovely on you, and quite festive. I love the jewel colors on you, but what will you wear with it?"

Zadie walked to a small chest, opened it, and removed her ruby earbobs. "Poppa gave these to me when I graduated."

"Yes, they will be wonderful with your dress. I only wish there was a real dowry to give Duncan, and not just that tiny amount your father left for you."

"Momma. Duncan does not care about my money. He'll allow me to keep what is mine."

"I never heard of such a thing. Do you not want your husband to handle your money?"

"It's not only my money, it is yours, and Abilene's. I am capable of handling the money." She stepped to where her mother was standing and kissed her. But when Zadie looked out the window, she remembered

Duncan was working. "Momma, I want to see if I can be of help to Duncan."

"What can you do?"

"I have no idea, but I want him to know that I'm supporting him and his efforts."

"I thought I managed to raise you to be a lady. I think I failed because you cling to that little child in you who wanted to run wild."

"Oh, Momma, don't worry. I'm not Catherine. She was afraid to swing too high for fear she'd fall. I wanted to reach the moon and the stars." She walked out of her bedroom. "I've never changed and I doubt that I ever will."

A few moments later, she found Duncan in the barn working with a length of pipe. He smiled when he saw her.

"Bored in the house?"

"Never. I can find all sorts of things to do with my spare time, but I wanted to see what I

could do for you. If I could be of any help...
Seems you only ask when you are desperate,
so I have come to offer."

"Thanks, I appreciate your willingness,
but there's nothing you can do. I've cut the
bent pipe away and now I must replace it.
Then I must straighten the blades."

"May I help?"

"Zadie." He shook his head. "There's
nothing I'd like more than someone who can
make this job go faster. But what could you
possibly do?"

"Straighten the blades. I know a little about
metal, because I had some sculpture classes."

He grinned. "That's more than I have
had. I know how to put on a metal roof." He
put down his wrench. "Will you ever stop
surprising me? You'll need a hammer."

"I need a ball peen."

He took the blades off the center ring

and set them aside. Then he found a hammer. "If you can do this, you'll save me a few hours of work. Use this bench."

She had been taught how to bend metal, not unbend it, and she had eighteen not-so-little blades stacked beside her. Some were mangled more than others. She knew where he kept some rags, so she grabbed a few and returned to the workbench. Picking up the first blade, she wondered how she was going to make it usable. Her fingers tightened on the handle of the ball-peen hammer and she studied the blade. They won't be pretty, but with luck, they will be functional.

After two hours of hearing the hammer hit metal, she needed a break from the ringing in her ears. She needed earplugs. She put down the hammer and went into the house. Abilene had a pot of stew on the stove, which smelled delicious.

"It's about time you came in from the cold." Abilene fixed her a bowl of stew.

"Do we have any beeswax?"

Abilene shook her head. "Only some candles."

"That will have to do." She took the proffered bowl and ate the stew. Then she poked around until she found a large old cup. "I'll take some to Duncan as soon as I finish trying to make some earplugs."

"Is that you making that horrible racket?"

She nodded.

Abilene melted the wax and Zadie managed to create something she could stuff in her ears to deaden the noise. They weren't great, but they helped. She wondered how some men managed to work with metal all day, but she also knew that many an older man was almost deaf.

Taking a cup of stew with her, she

returned to the barn and handed it to Duncan.

He slurped it down and thanked her. As the daylight began to fade, Duncan joined her. Between the two of them, they managed to repair the last few blades.

"With luck, we'll have water in a few minutes."

It took more than a few minutes. But Zadie watched how he put the whole thing back together, and she helped hoist the sails to the top of the tower. With her heart in her throat, she waited until he was finished bolting everything in place. Then he moved away, told her to release the rope, and watched as the blades began to rotate. Something protested with a squeal, and it didn't turn as smoothly as before, but it turned.

"Is it working?"

Duncan held his palms up. "Let's find out."

***

The spigots in the barn sputtered, burped, and burped some more. Duncan looked at Zadie and grimaced. "We're done for the night. I'll figure it out in the morning. The well probably needs to be primed."

He looked at Zadie as they walked to the house. She didn't look as though she would know what to do with a hammer, much less how to use one. Her delicate features hid her strong, capable, and willing fiber. How did I get so lucky?

Certainly his father only knew she was from a good family, educated, and pretty. He had no way of knowing she had become a woman with fortitude. Duncan smiled to himself when he took her hand. As they neared the back porch, he stopped and pulled her to him.

"I love you, Zadie Larkford, and I can't wait until the day we marry." His lips found hers.

When he broke his kiss, she answered, "Christmas Eve, Mr. Lorde. A church wedding with as many of your neighbors who will read the notice."

"What? I didn't dream that?"

She shook her head. "No. I surmised that you were too exhausted. But if I can't go to town and post the invitations to our wedding, I'm afraid we won't have anyone in attendance."

He kissed her again, and this time, he picked her up and spun her around. "You've made me the happiest man on this earth."

They both stopped long enough to listen to the windmill's squeal as the blades turned and hesitated in the slight breeze.

"Do you know what's wrong with it?"

Duncan shook his head. "Not exactly. The sails are no longer perfect."

"I tried. But some of the metal is in

terrible shape."

"Oh, darling, it's not your fault. You've saved me from hours of work or weeks without water until a replacement arrives. If the sails work, I don't care if it squeals." He took her hand and they walked onto the back porch. "We'll make it work. I promise by tomorrow this time, you will have running water."

She smiled up at him. "Yes. By working together, we will do well."

"I don't know how long it will take me to get the water running tomorrow, but I'll take you into town when the job is completed."

They stepped into the kitchen. Abilene was gone, but a small pot of stew sat on the counter along with several rolls.

"Tea?" Zadie asked, as she poured some water into a small pan.

Duncan nodded. An ewer of water sat near the sink and they both washed their hands. They ate their meal and then had what Abilene called poor man's wheels, rolled pieces of leftover pie dough had been flavored with cinnamon and sugar and then rolled, sliced, and baked. Duncan assumed that tomorrow's meal probably included some pies. Having Abilene was worth ten times what he spent at the dry goods and butcher shops, for her cooking was delicious. It seemed that every meal was fit for a king.

He and Zadie sat at the table for quite a while chatting. He'd never imagined that his life could be this good. He had a woman who was a partner and was also a friend. There was plenty more that he wanted and more that he needed. But when he gazed into her dark eyes, he knew they would not only survive as a couple, they would be successful. He only needed to marry her and have a son to carry his name onward.

The evening before Christmas Eve, Duncan ran up the steps to his room and retrieved a small box from a drawer. He carefully undid the old latch and lifted the lid. Inside was a locket that had once belonged to his grandmother. The locket was about the size of a silver dollar and made from solid gold. In the center was a small diamond. The box also contained a gold ring that matched the locket.

He opened the locket and removed the inner frame. With his penknife, he cut a small piece of paper to fit the interior. After fitting the paper into the locket, he replaced the frame. He carefully drew a heart on the tiny paper. Inside the heart, he wrote Z.L. & D.L. and under it he wrote the date of their wedding.

It took him longer than he expected, but he didn't care. He wanted Zadie to have something special. When he was certain the ink was dry, he closed the locket and polished it against the flannel of his shirt. Someday, Zadie, I'll buy you something bright and shiny. He checked the clasp on the heavy gold chain and rubbed the chain against his shirt. When he was satisfied, he put the ring and the locket in his pocket.

Downstairs, he found Zadie working on a painting in the room she called his office, but it contained her easel and other supplies.

"Any chance I can steal you away for a few moments?"

She looked up at him and smiled. "May I finish what I'm doing?"

He shrugged. "I'll only keep you for a minute or two."

She wiped her brush on a piece of cloth and stood. "Then I'm yours."

"Zadie, I want tomorrow to be special

for you."

"It will be. Momma and Abilene have made certain it will be grand."

He lowered his gaze to the brown, beige, and black rug. "You didn't give me much time to prepare for a lavish wedding. And in many ways, I've been amiss in my preparation for marriage. I'd like to fix some of that now."

He took Zadie's hands into his and dropped to one knee. "Will you marry me, because you love me and not just because…because there are so many other reasons to marry?"

Tears welled in her eyes and flowed over her cheeks. "Yes, I love you. I want to be your wife and give you children."

He grinned and pulled himself to his full height. "Do you still want a dozen?"

"Can we take that one at a time?"

"Why don't you take this for the time being?" He reached in his pocket and withdrew the locket. "It was my grandmother's."

She accepted the locket and examined it for a moment.

"Open it!"

She did and smiled. "Yes, Duncan Lorde, it is perfect for now and forever."

He reached into his pocket again and withdrew the ring. "I don't know if it will fit your finger."

He passed her the ring.

She slipped it on her finger, but it was too small. "She must have been tiny." She tried the ring on her pinky and it fit fine. "I will proudly wear it on my little finger."

"Then I will place it on that finger tomorrow. After the cattle have gone to market, I will buy you a beautiful ring that fits your wedding finger, something extravagant that shimmers in the sunlight."

"I don't need such a ring. I only need

your arms around me every day for as along as I live."

"Put your paints away, Zadie, and share my bed tonight. I'll keep you in my embrace for the entire night."

She giggled. "We've managed this long. There's no reason why we can't wait until tomorrow night."

Duncan groaned, but wrapped his arms around her and pulled her tight to his body as his lips found hers. He pressed tiny kisses all the way to her ear. "Don't ever change, Zadie. I like you just the way you are."

***

Zadie, her mother, Abilene, and Duncan rode into town on the day of Christmas Eve. Duncan stopped by the post office and handled all the normal things, while Abilene hurried to the butcher's. Then Zadie's mom and Abilene spent a few minutes in the dry goods store, choosing a few extra things that they needed, knowing they would receive guests during the holidays. Sitting in the buckboard waiting for everyone to finish their errands was the most difficult thing, for Zadie had wanted to join her mother and Abilene for their weekly shopping. But Zadie's mother, under the circumstances, forbid it and made Zadie stay in the buckboard. Then, a few minutes after three o'clock, they all headed over to the church. The old pastor chatted with them while Zadie helped set up the plates and Duncan carried the cake to the table at the back of the church.

Duncan remarked that he had never seen such a tall cake. It was decorated in bows made from icing. Beside it rested two sponge cakes rolled with a sweetened cream filling and berry jelly. Abilene had prepared more than enough food. Then she had worried and fussed the entire time, as she feared something would happen as they transported everything into town.

Zadie felt extra pretty in her festive dress. The bodice was made of velvet in her favorite shade of blue and piped in the silk plaid of her skirt. It was a bold plaid of blues and greens, with touches of ruby red on a white background. She had worn it once; last Christmas for a party her father had hosted. A warm flush of memories enveloped her as she remembered that cheerful evening.

Flowers were a must at a wedding, but none were available this time of year. Instead, Abilene had made her a nosegay of greenery and berries, and then tied it all with a red ribbon she had purchased at the dry goods store. Zadie loved it and thought it was perfect for the occasion.

The pastor lit the candles in the chandelier and the wall sconces. The church looked plain compared to the church that her family attended in Franklin. An oil lamp sat on the table near the cake. The pastor lit two more lamps in the front of the church. When he was done, he shooed Zadie into the tiny living quarters attached to the church.

By four o'clock, Zadie's mother came into the pastor's tiny parlor to say only a few people had come, but most of the merchants that had business dealings with Duncan had wives that came. At four-thirty, there were eighteen people in the tiny church.

Since there was no piano, Abilene merely told Zadie that the time had come before scooting away. Zadie took a few deep breaths and opened the door that led to the back of the tiny church. Duncan stood there in his suit and his beard was shaved. He offered her his hand and she took it.

"When did you get rid of the beard?" she whispered.

He winked and whispered back. "I have my ways. My mother would have a fit if she thought I was married while wearing a beard."

"You look so handsome without it."

She was officially trading her comfortable life in Franklin for her new one with Duncan in Creed's Crossing. She looked into Duncan's eyes and knew she was making the right decision. Together they would face their future, carve a livelihood out of a harsh territory, raise a family, and at the end of each day, she would find the warm, protective embrace of a loving man who cared about her.

Did you enjoy reading *A Rancher's Dream*
by E. Ayers?

Please leave a short review on your favorite platform and tell your friends! Independent authors count on your reviews to help them succeed. You can write to the author directly at the following website: http://www.ayersbooks.com

About the Author

Born and raised with wealth, E. Ayers turned away from all of it and married a few days after turning eighteen, to the shock and dismay of family and friends.

A firm believer in love conquering everything, there was never cause to look back. The newlyweds' life-long love became the springboard for many future novels.

Fascinated with the way people deal with everyday problems, E. Ayers has always been an observer and a listener. A simple problem for one person is a mountain for another. Utilizing those common predicaments, the subsequent novels have touched many lives.

Today finds E. Ayers writing while living in a pre-Civil War home with a dog and a cat. Rattling around in an old money pit provides one's muse with plenty of freedom. A perfect day is spent at the keyboard, coffee in hand, and everything in the house actually working as it should.

As the official matchmaker for all the characters who wander through a mind full of imagination and the need to share, E. Ayers enjoys finding just the right ones to create a story.

More Great Books From E. Ayers!

Wanting (A River City Novel)

A New Beginning (A River City Novel)

A Challenge (A River City Novel)

Forever (A River City Novel)

A Son (A River City Novel)

A Child's Heart (A River City Novel)

Coming Out of Hiding (a novel)

A Fine Line (a novella) *

Mariners Cove (a novella)

Ask Me Again (a novella)

A Skeleton at Her Door (a novella)

A Snowy Christmas in Wyoming (a novella) *

A Cowboy's Kiss in Wyoming (a novella) *

A Love Song in Wyoming (a novella) *

A Calling in Wyoming (a novella) *

Sweetwater Springs Christmas

(anthology) *

*Sweet Reads

YOU CAN VISIT CREED'S CROSSING AGAIN... AND AGAIN!

Please enjoy this peek into
A Snowy Christmas in Wyoming,
a novella from E. Ayers.

Caroline Coleman hadn't seen the place look this good since she was a teen. The flowerbeds were mulched and tidy. There was a new coat of green paint on the shutters and front door. Garlands of fresh pine wrapped the porch rails that encircled the log house, and a pretty, matching, pine wreath hung on the front door.

She knocked once and opened the door. "Grandmamma. It's me! I'm home."

"Thank goodness, you're here," a voice from a distant room called back. "I was worried about you coming in with this snowstorm on its way."

The stress of her journey slipped from her shoulders as she breathed in the familiar scent of home. Caroline let go of her rolling suitcase and looked around. Inside, everything looked the same, even though it was decorated for the holiday. A beautiful Douglas fir tree, covered with ornaments, stood in front of the window. Its tiny lights twinkled as if they were welcoming her.

The house was neater, cleaner, and there was a basket of toys next to the sofa. But everything else was exactly the way it had been all of her life. That familiarity wrapped her in a warm blanket.

"Darling, I'm so glad you're here. You're needed. This storm is going to be bad," Barbara Coleman said.

Caroline turned to her grandmother. The woman was holding a toddler whose eyes were filled with tears.

"What are you doing? Babysitting?" She hugged her grandmother and offered to take the child, but the child clung to the older woman.

"I guess you could call it babysitting. I'm trading, and I got the best end of this bargain. This is Sarah Anne Coyote. Isn't she a cutie?" Barbara took the child to a highchair in the kitchen. "Coffee?"

"Thanks. I'll get it. How did you wind up with a child?"

"Long story. You remember Margaret Simpson?" The older woman started fixing a snack.

"Double T ranch, of course."

"Her kids are selling everything since she died. Remember when I told you I was buying some of her land?" She put a handful of baby carrots on a plate, and stuck them in the microwave.

"Yes." Caroline poured a cup of coffee, then watched her grandmother fix a cup of milk with a sipping lid, and hand it to the toddler.

The child's enormous chocolate brown eyes were still washed in unshed tears and her long eyelashes were clumped with moisture. Chubby hands grabbed at the handles on the sippy-cup and tipped the cup of milk to her mouth. She watched Caroline with a reserved curiosity.

"Are you thirsty? Did you just wake up from a nap?" Caroline asked the child.

Little Sarah pursed her lips and banged on the tray in front of her. "Milk."

"How old is she? She's adorable. She's got the prettiest eyes."

"Thirteen months. She's a little handful. She's really coming out of her shell since she's been here." Barbara put several crackers spread with cheese on the child's tray. "Eat, sweet baby. You like creamed cheese." The microwave beeped and Barbara lifted the plate of baby carrots off the unit's carousel and put them on the child's tray after checking each one. "She's such a good thing. Just never thought I'd be playing with a baby at my age."

"Why did you nuke her carrots?"

"It slightly softens them. Makes them easier to eat. She doesn't have all her teeth."

"Grandmamma, you still haven't told me how you've wound up with a child."

"Well, I'm buying the eastern portion of Margaret's land, which includes her house and barn because it backs up to mine."

"Nice house."

"Yes, it is. I'm hoping to rent it. The one barn is in perfect shape, but the other barn has some problems and that's going to take more money."

Caroline rolled her eyes. Sarah giggled.

"Anyway, when Margaret died, her foreman lost his job."

"Oh, no. Sarah is one of those Coyotes?"

The back door opened and Andy Coyote walked into the kitchen. "Miz Barbara…"

Caroline stared at Andy. He wasn't the scrawny kid she'd known most of her life, and if it hadn't been for the scar across his cheek, she wouldn't have recognized him. His shoulders were broad and he'd grown very tall. The long straight nose, strong cheekbones, and his coloring conveyed his Crow Indian heritage, except he was taller than most.

"Excuse me, I didn't know you had company." He took his jacket off and hung it on the peg by the back door.

"Company? I doubt that anyone would call me company," Caroline shot back at him.

She couldn't remember the last time she'd seen him, maybe high school.

He looked at her for a brief second, then grabbed a mug, and poured a cup of coffee.

"Caroline, you remember Andy?" Barbara asked.

"How could I not remember Andy?" Memories of the young man and his family flowed through her brain like a bad news story.

Sarah squealed with delight as Andy took her in his arms. "How's my baby girl?"

The child pointed to Caroline.

"Yes, that's Caroline," Andy said with a big grin. "Have you been playing with her? I thought you just got up from your nap."

"She did just get up from her nap as Caroline came through the door. I brought her in here for her snack. She hasn't had a chance to play."

He pulled his mobile phone from his pocket and looked at it. "We're in trouble."

"What kind of trouble?" Barbara asked as she cleaned up the crumbs off the child's tray and handed the toddler the last tiny carrot. "Are you talking about the storm?"

Andy turned on the TV and watched the weather channel. "I've been watching the storm track on my phone. I'm gonna need help getting that herd down here. I can't do it alone. If I can find help, I'll leave tonight. That is if you don't mind keeping Sarah for me."

Barbara turned to her granddaughter. "Caroline'll go with you."

Andy turned around and stared hard. "You? You think you can ride herd?"

"Darn right, I can ride. Won't be the first herd I've ever brought in, but I..." She bit her tongue.

"But what?"

She forced a smile. "Let's just say I always

ride with a gun, and I know how to use it."

"Good. So do I. We'll leave at six. Make sure you're saddled and ready to go."

Hot anger boiled through Caroline. "I'll be ready."

She stormed out of the kitchen, grabbed her suitcase, and headed for her room.

***

"She'd better be able to ride. This isn't going to be an easy cattle drive," Andy said.

"That little thing knows every square inch of this ranch and this business. My husband used to say, 'Let her go, and when she's done, she'll come back.' I hope he was right."

"Ma'am, I don't need a prissy female. I need a man for this job or I'll never get that herd back here."

"Oh, she can do it. She and her grandfather

moved herds all the time. She's knows what she's doing and she knows this land. Listen to her."

Andy kissed his daughter's nose and put her to the floor. "Are you sure you can handle her overnight?"

"I can handle your daughter overnight." Barbara laughed. "Just don't try to handle my granddaughter, or she'll be bringing you back in a sack."

"Miz Barbara, one female in my life is plenty. I don't need anymore."

***

Caroline cinched the saddle and adjusted the stirrups before tying on her pack. Her mind drifted over the stories of Jessie and Clare Coleman and the things that they endured to start this ranch in the 1840's. She had vowed to write their story one day. Clare was barely fifteen when she married Jessie and went west with him. The handwriting in that diary was difficult to decipher, but Caroline managed to read it when she was a teen. Snowstorms were nothing new, and if Jessie and Clare could survive them, there was no reason why she couldn't do it today. Except instead of doing it with her grandfather at her side, she had Andy Coyote. She grimaced as bile rose from her stomach.

"You ready to ride, Caroline?" Andy asked.

"Yes, I'm ready." She pulled her scarf over her head and shoved her old felted Stetson over the hot pink angora.

"Don't wimp out on me. I need another man for this job, not a fancy Washington, D.C. TV news anchor."

"Well, I have a job to do, and the idea of having you along for the ride has no appeal. As far as I'm concerned, you're strictly brawn, and you'd better do as I say."

"This is gonna be hell," he mumbled as he yanked on his horse's reins.

"That's right, and don't forget it." Caroline put her foot into the stirrup.

Caroline pulled her scarf tighter around her face. An occasional snowflake floated down as they rode. She wasn't going to let on that she was dead tired, but she was certain that if she'd blink her eyes, they wouldn't open again. She had worked yesterday doing the six and eleven o'clock nightly news broadcasts, and then caught an early morning flight out of D.C. Three hours of sleep was not enough.

"Caroline!"

She gasped and righted herself.

"You're falling asleep."

She looked over at Andy and frowned.

"If you talked to me, you might stay awake," he suggested.

"What would you like to discuss?" she snarled.

He chuckled. "You want my opinion on the Senate's newest budget?"

"Oh, save your breath."

"I didn't think so. Why don't you tell me what it's like living in the big city and having a hotshot job?"

"Nothing to tell. I have a condo overlooking the Potomac River. I have a driver who takes me to and from work. The clothes I wear are chosen by someone else, even my hair is styled according to the network's consultant, and I don't have a say so in any of it."

"I think you look mighty pretty. Miz Barbara and I always watch you while we eat our dinner."

"Why are you living in the house with my grandmother?"

"And not living in the foreman's

apartment in the barn?"

"Yes." The idea of a Coyote living under her grandmother's roof bothered her. As far as she was concerned they were all filthy criminals.

The only sounds were theirs, the horses' breaths, the soft slap of leather reins, and the thumping of hooves on the frozen earth. Finally he answered, "She didn't want me out there in that small apartment with the baby. She thought it was easier on Sarah if I stayed in the house."

"Where's Sarah's mom?"

"Don't know and don't care." He nudged his horse to pick up the pace.

"Nice attitude."

"Yours sucks, too."

"I don't have a child," she retaliated.

"I have two. I'm not allowed near my son."

She shook her head. "What did you do to prevent visitation?"

"Fathered the boy."

"How old is he?"

"He'll be fifteen in February."

Her mind spun back in time to Andy and Katelyn as teens. They were inseparable. The fun loving, petite female with wide set eyes had always been a fierce competitor in 4H and was an amazing trick rider. Then Katelyn vanished. "So the rumors were true?"

"Half true. I never raped her. We were kids and thought we were in love. When she found out she was pregnant...her dad came looking for me with a rifle in his hand. Three years later, the judge threw it all out. I was forced to sign an order to stay away from Katelyn and my son."

Somehow she understood the wealthy family's rage. She could also imagine Katelyn's tears at being torn from the boy she loved. But Andy was a Coyote, and those boys were hellions. "She still here?"

"If you mean still in the county, no. According to a few friends, she's living outside of Boulder, raising horses, and happily married to some hotshot lawyer."

"And your son?"

"He's with her. She'll tell him the truth someday."

"What about Sarah?"

"Another big mistake. Sarah's not, but her mom was. I'll be honest. My life was a mess. I was living in Casper when I meet Jessica. We went out a few times and then we started living together. She was hot. Then one day she tells me that she's pregnant. Two weeks later, the warehouse where I'd been working closed. I started searching for any job I could find."

Andy's momentary silence hung in the cold air.

Caroline straightened her back and rolled her shoulders. Fatigue was robbing her body, but she wanted him to keep talking. He was right. Conversation kept her awake.

"It was a bad situation. I needed money and there were no jobs. Eventually, I found a job working back here for Double T. They needed a hand. But Jessica didn't want to come. She wanted to live in the city. Had a big fight. I tried a half dozen times to patch things up. Then the phone quit working and my envelopes were returned with no forwarding address. When Margaret Simpson died, her kids kicked everyone out and started selling everything off. I got lucky and got a part-time job working at Kalab's Store."

"Doing what?"

"Anything. Didn't matter to me. It was a job. Had to cover the payment on my truck and put food in my belly. That's where I found your grandmother. She was complaining to BillieJo Kalab about not being able to do everything. That evening I came out to her house. I begged for a job and a place to sleep."

"My grandmother does not complain about anything."

"Well, call it whatever you want, but those two women were commiserating about how hard life was."

"Oh, big word."

"Knock it off, Caroline. Just 'cause I didn't run off to some big university in Virginia doesn't make me an idiot."

She nudged her horse. "You never were an A student."

"No, I wasn't. But you don't have to get uppity with me."

She looked over at him. "You calling me a snob?"

"I really don't care what you are, as long

as you can get this herd back to where I can take care of them. Your grandmother doesn't need to lose her livestock because they've frozen to death."

She hid her snarl. "So how did you wind up with Sarah?"

"I'd been here about three weeks when Miz Barbara got a phone call. Seems Social Services tracked me down. Sarah had been abandoned. She was in bad shape. If it weren't for your grandmother...I don't know what I'd do."

"She's adorable."

"She is. I'll do anything to make sure nothing ever happens to her again."

Ask for A Rancher's Woman, A Creed's Crossing Historical at your favorite local bookseller today. Available in Large Print!